Red Card
The Detroit Black Jacks Book 1
Liz Crowe

This is a work of fiction. Similarities to real people, places, or events are entirely coincidental.

RED CARD

First edition. May 6, 2024.

Copyright © 2024 Liz Crowe.

ISBN: 979-8224755905

Written by Liz Crowe.

To second chances,
no matter what form they take

"This is our business, guys. You gotta learn it now so you can run it for me someday," Melanie said for the millionth time as she watched her youngest son, Tanner, wrap silverware in napkins, a big smile on his face. Her other son, Zach, was showing much less enthusiasm for his family business duty — bussing tables — on a busy Saturday morning.

The business in question was Ayden's Café, her instantly popular and successful breakfast and lunch café. She'd sailed past their honeymoon first year into a second with rave reviews among townies and college types alike. She ran it with a firm, fair hand, and made both her sons work as many hours as they could manage.

Tanner, an energetic pre-teen, never complained and even asked for more tasks. Zach despised it, making no secret of the fact that his soccer-playing career and his social life had been eviscerated by his mother's stupid restaurant that had uprooted them from Grosse Pointe to the college town west of Detroit. They hadn't spoken much beyond the basics for the entire time they'd lived here. He even kept some of his clothes in boxes in his room and spent the entire summer furiously filling out college applications to places as far from Michigan as he could get.

"How will I pay for this?" she'd demanded earlier in the week, watching as he hit send for schools in Florida, Colorado, and California.

"Scholarships, Mom. You've talked to the coaches already, or are you too busy serving eggs to everyone in town but us to remember?" She'd opened her mouth to berate him but snapped it shut, realizing he was speaking the truth. She had poured everything she had into Ayden's Café during its startup year, thankful for the distraction and for her father, who'd more or less forced her into taking on the project.

She'd slumped against his door frame, sick of all the negativity and fighting, but without a lick of energy to conjure a rebuttal. Zach brushed past her. "Don't worry. I handled it. I sent them all schedules for this last season coming up, and DVDs of my old team. You don't have to do anything," he stated in a flat voice, waving away his younger brother who'd materialized at the sound of an argument.

Tanner worshipped his older brother and always had. The boys had been close but Zach was withdrawing from him now, too, which broke her heart. She tried not to have a favorite. But god help her, Zachary was impossible and had been his whole life. Tanner was calm, accommodating, and always willing to give her a hug. She was pretty sure she hadn't felt her older son's arms around her since he was seven or eight years old.

Leaving the crowded dining area, she headed for her office, a cluttered space in a single room over the café. She sat and touched the talismanic photo of her and her sister. Alicia had been girl-next-door pretty. Blonde, athletic, funny, easygoing, so comfortable in her own skin, which drove Mel mad with jealousy even while she did all the caretaker stuff for her—breakfasts, lunches, dinners, driving her to soccer practices so many times she believed her car could drive the route on its own.

Mel had never felt pretty, although she was told it enough. She simply considered herself Alicia's eternal caretaker. So, when she'd looked up from her part-time job at the bank all those years ago to discover Scott Miller, manager of private banking, staring at her as if she were a mirage, something had clicked inside her head. Something stupid, she now realized, and something she'd never heed again. It wasn't love. It was need. Her need to be loved. Her desire to be something other than "Alicia's sister."

That life had imploded within a few years, leaving her the divorced mom of two boys living with her father in her childhood home in Grosse Pointe. And then that playboy athlete had swooped into their lives, screwing with Alicia's priorities and whisking her far away. Mel had been not only jealous all over again, but pissed. She'd missed her sister during the years she'd spent gallivanting around the world, getting her picture taken as the pretty wife of Metin Sevim, mother of his adorable little boy and not the star soccer player she'd worked so hard to become.

Before she would allow herself the pleasure of a good cry, another photo caught her eye. One of Zach in his soccer uniform, leg drawn back ready to score a goal. His dark blond hair and blue eye made him look like his father, but the attitude and stubbornness all hers. Face flushed, she turned back to her laptop screen and the seemingly innocuous email filling the screen. The email she'd been reading over and over for the last few hours now felt seared into her retinas. Her world reduced to a pinprick of light, centered on the device that seemed almost superfluous there, amongst the coffee and toast-scented new reality of her life.

"Hey, Mel! You've got a visitor."

"Oh, um, thanks." She smiled at the server who'd run up the short flight of stairs to find her, and shut the computer, heart pounding so hard it hurt. She'd gotten the message. Someone was trying to find him—Metin—and for reasons that totally escaped her, that someone was asking for her help. Apparently, this person had not received the memo that, as far as she was concerned, that man had moved out of her life forever and thank god for that. Just seeing his name in an email made her eyes burn with fury and loss.

Using her newly developed powers of detection, she noted that tables three and seven had empty coffee cups, so she grabbed the pot to do some refills, smiled at a few regulars, waved to another and made her way to the front of the café. Her back ached and her feet were sore—par for her course lately. Her mind spun with budgets, staffing, and food-ordering dramas. But she'd never been happier. Until that morning, of course, when an email from a total stranger had ripped the never-quite-healed scab off the memory of her sister and nephew.

One of the bartenders shouted her name. She stopped to solve his problem, then turned and came face to face with the tall, be-suited form of a man who looked like he stepped off an advertisement for "don't you wish your husband looked like this?" At his side stood another good-looking guy, dressed in jeans and a T-shirt emblazoned with a poker chip, the letters BJG embroidered above it. She sucked in a breath. Ignoring that email had officially become impossible.

The suit stuck out a hand. "Hi, Melanie Miller, right? I'm Jack, Jack Gordon. I sent you an email yesterday."

She froze. Her brain fogged over with fury that he dared to come into her café and confront her this way while she made a show of not taking his outstretched palm. Lifting her chin and crossing her arms, Mel studied his face, silently demanding an explanation. Jack Gordon kept his gaze neutral.

"Melanie, I'm Rafael Inez," the other man spoke. "I played with your brother-in-law once. And I followed his career. So please let me say how sorry...."

She held up a hand. "Ex-brother-in-law, you mean. What do you want?" She knew damn well what they wanted, of course. She hated the sound of her own voice, but these guys were dragging the whole nightmare of her loss out into the light of day, and forcing her to take a long, deep sniff of its stink. She had no time or desire to do that, much less discuss the man she blamed for it.

"Can we sit, talk?" Rafe asked.

She glared at his too-hot-for-his-own-good face.

"No. Sorry. I'm busy."

"We need to get in touch with him, with Metin. His agent dropped him, as you probably know, and his parents won't respond to our requests. I just thought...." Rafael shrugged.

"I don't know where he is. You can go now." She took another step away from them.

"I realize this is hard for you, but we only want to talk to him about a job."

"It doesn't matter to me what you want him for. I don't know where he is, nor do I care."

Rafe gestured toward the picture she had on the wall above the front window of her sister with Ayden. The photo had been taken—by Metin, no doubt—as they sat on his parents' veranda. The European side of Istanbul was spread out in panorama behind them. The boy's dark eyes were alight as he stared up at his mother. And Alicia was radiant, as always.

They were forever frozen for Mel that way, and she sent up a small prayer of forgiveness to them both every day. Letting that visual cancel out the two that remained lodged in her brain, how they'd looked the last time she'd seen them both.

"Listen, Melanie, you really are our last hope for this. You honor your sister's memory every day, and her son's every time you open your doors here. I'm not asking you to do anything more than that. Alicia wouldn't want Metin's talent wasted the way he's done for the last two years, and you know it. We need him to come help us run the Detroit soccer team, to offer him a shot at something new."

She wrestled with familiar demons, keeping her face calm the entire time. On the one hand, her sister would hate her for being so aloof, for refusing to speak to Metin, or his parents, whom Mel liked. She knew damn good and well that withdrawing from him completely, taking her sons and father with her, had sent the man even deeper into despair. But she was only protecting herself.

"Last I heard, he was in his condo in Madrid," she ground out, hating that she even cared enough to lie. "Hiding and drinking and whoring and whatever else. This, of course, after he showed up at my sister's and nephew's funeral drunk." She touched her nose, as the ghost of memory about how that particular day had traversed the spectrum from horrific to somehow worse.

"He isn't there. We were sort of hoping...." Rafe ran a hand through his hair.

Anger replaced the tiny bit of remorse she'd allowed herself in a split second. "You honestly think I'm going to reach out to the man? After all this time and what he did... to my... I mean...." She averted her eyes, tears threatening. This was her life, her business, and she had no intention of doing anything to upset it by yanking that man back into it.

"Melanie." Jack the Suit's deep voice startled her. She swiped her eyes, glaring at them both. "I know this sounds like all kinds of sneaky and unfair, but I think even you would admit that it's time for him to move on, to have a life. You've got one, I see, and a successful one at that." He gestured at the busy café around them. "We want him to coach our new expansion team. We're building a new stadium, have already recruited players."

She laughed, an ugly sound that made her wince at the same time. "You honestly think I give a shit about your soccer team?" She was having a tough time catching her breath. The nerve of these men.

"Alicia wouldn't want him to..."

"Stop right there." Her voice broke on the last word, betraying her. "You have no right to come into my place of business and say a single word about my sister to me. Not one..."

"Alicia?"

She winced, hearing a familiar voice from somewhere behind her. She was suddenly aware that her voice was raised to a level that pretty much everyone could hear, and pretty much everyone had stopped what they were doing to listen to her. She sucked in a long breath, glared at the two men, then turned to face her father.

"You sent them here." She didn't frame it as a question.

"I did. Good to see you again, Jack. Rafe." He shook the men's hands while she fumed. When he turned to face her, she was startled to note how much he'd aged. Since she didn't see him every day like she had for so many years spent living in the big house in Grosse Pointe with her kids, it shouldn't surprise her, but it did. She touched his suit lapel. "Dad, I'm not... I can't..." He took her hand.

"You don't have to do anything you don't want to do, Melanie. Jack's a friend from college and he reached out to me to ask if it would be okay to contact you. I thought..." He sighed, patted her hand, then tucked it into his elbow and turned so they were both facing the other men. "Sorry. I guess she's not as ready as I thought she was."

Mel ground her teeth. She hated letting her father down. She yanked her hand away from the comforting crook of his arm and glared at the two men again.

"I think I still have his private cell number. I'll give it to you. I also have one of his brothers' numbers." She squeezed her eyes shut as memories rushed into her consciousness—from that whole hellish week after the accident, then the nightmare of a funeral. At some point, one of Metin's brothers—Timur, she thought she recalled his name—had pressed a card into her hand. She'd kept it for reasons unknown to her at the time.

"Um, actually...." Rafe smiled at her. She clenched her jaw against a flare of anger at him. Mainly because he reminded her of Metin with his deep brown skin, dark hair and deep brown gaze.

"Stop using the puppy dog eyes. I'm immune. Spit it out."

"We were hoping you would go see him in person."

She took a big step back, bumping up against her father. He put a hand on her shoulder, but she shook it off. "No. No way. Now, can I get you guys some coffee or breakfast? I need to get back to work."

Jack shot her a dazzling smile, blinding her for a split second with his perfection. She shook her head. "You must get into all kinds of trouble with the ladies."

"Nah, not anymore." He matched her stance, crossing his arms and shifting his weight to one leg. "Gave it all up for someone special and three kids." He paused, a frown marring his otherwise perfect features. "I know this is hard, and I'm sorry we have to make you dredge all of it up, but...."

"We'll pay your way to Madrid or Istanbul or wherever he's holed up. Honestly, I think the only thing that would drag him back to the land of the living, and make him willing to consider our offer, is to hear from you," Rafe said.

"You don't know me, and my supposed relationship with him, very well, do you?"

"All I know is what I've heard other people say about him in the last eighteen months or so. People close to him, including his ex-agent."

Mel raised an eyebrow, readying for the Melanie-is-a-raving-bitch stories.

"The rumors are that he misses the connection with Alicia's family. He's hurt that you won't talk to him anymore."

"He's a drunk, washed up former playboy who stole my sister and then got her killed." The sheer irrationality of what she said hardly registered. Her eyes blurred with tears. "Now get out, unless you're gonna eat."

"Melanie," her father said. She ignored him and spun away from them, pushing her way past a couple of servers to get upstairs to the relative quiet of her office. She slammed the door behind her before sliding to the floor and sobbing as if it had been only yesterday she'd identified her nephew's ruined body and had to watch her sister die right in front of her eyes a few days after that.

Finally, the tears dried up, and she sat at her desk, staring at a photo of her and Alicia at her sister's wedding. It was hard to square the resentment with the fierce, protective love she'd felt for her younger sister, all those years she'd spent more or less raising her after their mother died. Alicia had been her father's favorite from the moment she'd shown her tomboy tendencies, and he'd slapped her into a pair of soccer cleats. Her mother had enabled Melanie's girliness—the obnoxious pink bedroom, the closet full of clothes, the dance lessons—for as long as she could. But it didn't take long for Cathy Matthews to go from completely organized and in-charge, to limp with pain as the cancer ravaged its way through her system, and then comatose in order to avoid it.

Mel leaned back and attempted to drag a mental picture of her mother out from under all the years spent without her. She'd stepped up and handled Alicia's life, because she knew how hard her father worked not to show his desperate grief. Mel's life as pseudo-mom to her sister had felt like a burden some days, but a blessing on others. Until she'd had her own life blown apart by stupid choices once Alicia had been old enough to be on her own.

The visceral distaste she still harbored for Alicia's husband could probably be chalked up to pure jealousy that her sister found someone so much like their father. It was easier for her to blame Metin, to lash out and pick fights. She'd alienated them both with her behavior on more than one occasion, including that god awful Christmas.

She pressed her forehead onto the desk, willing to have it all back for another chance to talk to Alicia, to tell her she didn't mean to be unsupportive of her choice to be a mom and wife, to give up one dream for another. Hell, she'd even tolerate that sappy Turk for the chance to see Alicia again, to hold her nephew on her lap.

"I'm sorry, Alicia. I ruined our time together and now..." The sob broke from her chest as familiar anger barreled in behind the sadness. She could hear her sister's voice, her infernal, unreasonable devotion to the man who'd seduced her and knocked her up, as clear as if the woman were alive and standing beside her in the small office.

"Mel, you have to help him. He's still family. And he needs us. Please?

The sobs subsided, leaving her feeling empty in a way she hadn't felt since moving out of her father's house and opening her café. She kissed the photo of Alicia and opened the second-hand desk drawer. Timur Sevin's card was right there where she'd put it, as if it were a talisman, when she should have just pitched it into the garbage can. She turned it over, feeling the heft of it. Ran her fingertip across the embossed letters and numbers with an unfamiliar address and a phone number with a nine-zero in front of it for Turkey.

She knew where Metin was. She knew because Metin's mother kept in touch for reasons that were beyond her, but that Mel anticipated in some strange perversion of logic. But it was information that felt sacred, or best kept secret. Which was why she'd bald-faced lied to the men who'd come here thanks to her father's urging. The bottom line was that Metin had disappeared into a bottle in Turkey, not Spain, and hadn't emerged. The family was worried, terrified, resigned. So yeah, she knew exactly where he was, damn it.

Wiping her eyes, she headed downstairs and over to where the three men sat with platefuls of food and mugs of coffee in front of them. She caught her father's gaze first, then looked at the other two. "Metin's not in Madrid. He's in some flat by himself in Istanbul, his mother told me last week. I'll go talk to him. But I have my own conditions." She poked a finger into Rafe's shoulder. "If I help get him back here, you have to help my son find a way to play soccer in college. It's all he's ever wanted, for reasons that escape me. And he won't talk to me about it anymore. That's my deal."

Rafe rose so fast the other men had to grab their coffee mugs to avoid spilling, stuck out a hand for her to shake, his dark eyes full of emotion. "Thank you, Melanie. Give me your son's phone number. I'll call him today and get his schedule so I can come watch him play. Then we'll formulate a plan."

Jack Gordon sat smiling at her. She stood stock still, lest she give in to the urge to punch them both in the face for dragging Metin Sevim back into her life.

Her father got up from the table. But she held up her hand. "No, no, finish your breakfast. I... I have some phone calls to make."

Chapter Two

"**I** can take care of us, Mom. You don't need to make Granddad come all the way out here."

She hugged Zach as long as he would allow it—about three seconds—then kissed Tanner's cheek. "I'll take you next time, honey," she told him. "I need to go do this thing for Aunt Alicia."

"I want to see Metin," Tanner whined, still hovering around as she rechecked her purse for her passport, wallet, phone, and other stuff she was terrified of forgetting.

"Leave her alone," Zach snapped. "The sooner she leaves, the sooner we can invite all those people over we talked about."

Tanner wiped his eyes. "What people?"

She shot her oldest son a fierce glare. Zach leaned on the doorway to the kitchen. Tall, handsome, his face a mask of "I don't give a shit" so much like his father's she almost choked.

"I think it's great you're doing this, Mom," Tanner said.

"Suck up," Zach said under his breath, but he pulled his little brother close to his side, which made Tanner grin. "For the record, I don't."

"Oh?" Mel checked the time. It was exactly three and a half minutes since the last time she checked. Still a solid three hours before boarding. Then it dawned on her that Zach had spoken to her and in a way that didn't involve bored, pissed-off teenaged boy angst. She glanced at him. He had Tanner in a fake choke hold in one arm, which made the kid giggle and fake try to escape. But his blue eyes were narrowed. Dare she think he was concerned for her?

"Why not?" She kept her tone neutral. God knew the kids had seen her bitching and moaning enough, had been witness to plenty of arguments between her and Alicia's husband, and of course, the coup de grâce—that moment when she'd yelled at Metin about showing up drunk to the funeral and he'd shoved her out of his way, which made her stumble into a bunch of flowers and other mementos, fall, and land on her face, resulting in an immediate bloody nose and black eyes to match later that week. Embarrassment hit her square in the face, making her shudder.

"I thought he was out of our lives, Mom," Zach said. His use of the word "mom" threw her, especially the way he said it. She blinked fast to hide the emotion that threatened, wanting to yank him close for another hug. He let go of Tanner and crossed his arms, resuming his father's "well? What do you have to say for yourself?" stance.

Her youngest walked back to her. "Are you okay? Really?" She smiled and brushed his hair out of his eyes.

"I'm fine. It's fine. Your Grandad and I think it's time we…um…reconnect, I guess. But mostly I'm doing a favor for the soccer team guys."

"What soccer team?" Tanner looked confused and glanced at his big brother for an explanation.

Zach threw up his hands. "Whatever. You do you. Even though this is kind of a new you, when it comes to him, isn't it?"

"Yes, Zach it is. I was…" She paused, stumbling over the concept. "I was wrong to push him away. It wasn't his fault. It was… an accident." Her voice broke, but she'd cried enough tears in front of these boys. She cleared her throat.

To her utter shock, Zach took the three feet between them in a long stride and pulled her close. She found herself with her nose buried in his shoulder, Tanner's arms encircling her on the other side. She let it happen, because as soon as she made a big deal about it, he'd be mortified. When he let her go, his eyes were bright. "I love you," she said, putting her palm alongside his cheek. Her little boy, now practically a grown man. "And you," she said, turning to Tanner to let Zach off the hook.

"You love me more," he said, grinning at their old joke.

"That's right," she said.

"Great," Zach said, sniffling and heading to the kitchen. "So go already. You've got, what, three whole hours, so that should satisfy your need to be super early for the flight."

Her phone dinged with an alert that her ride share had arrived. "Right. Yes. Okay."

Tanner carried her small suitcase for her, gave her a quick squeeze, then ran back inside. She allowed herself a quick look at her house, their house, their home for the last almost two years, then ducked into the backseat before she burst into actual tears and freaked out the driver.

• • • •

THE PLANE TRIP WAS long and boring. Almost as long and boring as the hour and a half she had to wait to board. But she'd rather wait than rush, she kept reminding herself as she tapped out more text instructions to her café's manager.

Finally, after the poor woman had reminded her that she'd sent the same instructions twice, she put her phone away. Flying on the soccer club's dime meant she had a first-class seat, and she availed herself of the free booze for the first couple of hours. The memory of her last trip to Turkey for the wedding—also in first class thanks to Metin's family—slammed into her, making her heart ache. She stared out into the purple darkness high above the clouds somewhere over the ocean. What was she doing? Why did she even think she could help? She hated the man and everything he represented. She needed to be home, running her business, trying to convince her older son not to hate her guts. But the stuffy, uncomfortable-regardless-of-being-in-first-class plane kept flying.

She jolted awake when the wheels hit the tarmac, interrupting an odd dream about soccer matches featuring Zach and her ex-brother-in-law, with somehow alive Alicia and Ayden cheering in an otherwise completely empty stadium. She made her way through the airport in a daze, stopped to gulp water, then to pee, grateful she didn't have to bother with luggage since she'd packed light in a carry-on. Metin's mother—an imposing and striking woman in a chic black pantsuit, dark hair scraped back into a severe bun—spotted her first. At the sight of her, more unwanted memories flooded in. She closed her eyes, then opened them, determined not to let embarrassment or anything else get in the way of the mercy mission, or whatever the hell had brought her here.

"Melanie! Canim! I'm so happy to see you."

She accepted the woman's embrace. Feyza had lost a ton of weight and her face had lines Mel didn't recall. Shoving away the evil visions of the last time they'd been together at the funeral, she smiled and pulled away.

"I am mostly happily to be in here, to be seeing with you again," she managed in rudimentary Turkish.

Feyza burst out laughing. Mel frowned. A tall man in a dark suit took her suitcase and led the way out to a waiting Mercedes.

"I forgot you learned my language," she said, patting Mel's knee once they were ensconced in the back seat together. "So admirable. But you always were smart."

Her stomach flipped over as the driver lurched out into the exhaust-filled line of traffic. The discomfort level she always maintained around her sister's in-laws pressed in on her. So many memories were getting upturned like last year's garbage by the woman's presence, Mel nearly gagged on them.

"So, how is he?" she finally asked.

"My son is a crushed, ruined shell of himself. But you know that, I think."

Mel trained her gaze on the flat, industrial landscape around the airport as the woman kept talking, filling her in on Metin's failed attempt to play for one of the bigger Turkish teams since being cut from Real Madrid, then a lesser Spanish team. He'd played two games and gotten himself ejected with a red card after ten minutes into the second half for leaping up on an opposing player and pounding the other man nearly unconscious with his fists. It had fueled many a heated argument in the soccer world, the sad decline of one of their superstars. Mel hated it, hated him, and hated herself for coming here.

"I don't know what I can do really," she whispered to herself and the ghost of her sister, Alicia. "Why do you think I can help him?"

"I don't know if you can, my dear." Feyza's voice broke. "But when the men from the new club in America contacted me, I suggested they reach out to you. Because at this point, I'm willing to try anything."

"Mrs. Sevim, have you forgotten how we parted? The funeral? I know I haven't, and I doubt he has either." She tried to keep the frustration out of her voice.

The woman's dark eyes filled with tears. Mel bit back her urge to keep talking. It had been the worst possible ending, the most awful, drama-filled bullshit. With her and Metin at the core of it. She could still hear her own screams when Metin had shown up, drunk off his ass. She still felt the bright red rage she'd experienced, as if it had happened an hour and not two years ago.

That and the pain when her nose connected with the floor. An accident, but it hadn't helped matters, not one bit.

"No. I will never forget it. Nor will he. But you are here now, are you not? So you must think he is worth saving." The woman grabbed her hand and clenched it. "Please, try. For Alicia and Ayden's memory. This may be his last chance at something normal."

"I will. For them, and no one else," she said through clenched teeth. They were silent the rest of the way to the Sevim family estate.

Mel passed an awkward evening in the company of Metin's parents. Dinner with them, and Metin's two brothers and sisters-in-law, was subdued, but polite. Conversation topics included pretty much everything under the sun except the reason she sat there among them. The pariah, the bitchy sister of the woman their beloved son had adored and married. Thankfully, she didn't have to trot out her rusty Turkish. The Sevim family was three generations wealthy, most of them held international college degrees, and all of them spoke perfect, if slightly formal, English.

When the pressure building behind her eyes became too much, she finally interrupted the Sevim patriarch as he started talking about some financial crisis, making everyone stop and stare.

"So, where is he? I should go, I mean. To see Metin. To try to get him to agree to take a coaching job in America. I can't... I'm too...." She lowered her eyes. A tear hit her clenched hands.

There was a general, group throat clearing.

She glared at each of them in turn. "Listen, I realize we all parted badly. That funeral was god-awful, and I take my part in the responsibility for it. But he...." Her voice broke, pissing her off. "He didn't have to show up blind drunk, you know. I mean...."

"Melanie," Metin's father intoned. "We are as embarrassed by that as you were. It was unseemly and immature of him." Metin's oldest brother started to push his chair from the table. His father put a hand on his arm. "No, Bulent, you know I am right. Metin was, and still is, acting like a child. He must be the man he is meant to be. It is tragic and horrible, this thing that happened. But he has to move on now. If it takes moving to America to coach, so be it."

The older man paused, giving her a full glimpse of how hard this had hit him. It was crystal clear in the slump of his shoulders, the dark circles under his eyes, the hollowed out angles of his cheekbones. "He has ruined himself for playing in Europe. But football is the only thing he has. If it will save him, then we must try it." He took a sip of his tea. His dark, serious eyes mesmerized her. "I miss my grandson so much, I ache every day for him. So I can only imagine what Metin is feeling. He was—is—a very emotional boy and has let that rule him too much as a man. No matter how you, or I, or Metin's mother, felt about his marriage to your sister, we must now help him get past her loss." He rose, keeping his dark gaze on hers. "Please, excuse me."

Metin's brothers kept their eyes on their plates. Mel blinked, processing his last words. Metin's family had been so loudly supportive, so openly adoring of her sister. It shocked her to her core to find out they hadn't liked the arrangement any more than she had.

A wave of protectiveness rose in her. How dare they? Alicia was perfect, smart, talented, a wonderful mother. These people could all kiss her ass. She got to her feet.

"Okay, now that I know where we all stand. Will someone tell me where the man of the hour is, so I can find him and drag him into the light and then get back to my life?"

Timur, Metin's next oldest brother, the one who resembled him the most, got to his feet. "I'll take you there now."

Chapter Three

After a harrowing trip across one of the many bridges between the Asian and European sides of Istanbul, they pulled up to a glass and steel skyscraper in Etiler, one of the more exclusive neighborhoods on the European side of the Bosporus Straights. Mel sat, clutching the key card Metin's brother had handed her before driving her in utter silence across the bridge and fighting his way through traffic to this spot. They sat in the large SUV, getting honked at, until she took a breath and put her hand on the door handle.

"Good luck," Timur said, not meeting her eyes.

"Listen, I'm sorry about... everything, I guess." She wanted him to accompany her up to the top floor. But he seemed entrenched behind the wheel.

He finally met her gaze, the agony on his face clear. "Just get him out of there, if you can. Thanks."

She sat, frozen with indecision, fearful of facing Metin after so much time, and still unable to comprehend what these people thought she could do for him. "Why do you think he'll listen to me?" She addressed the windshield, sweat dripping down her back. "I mean, we didn't exactly part on good terms."

She'd be damned if she let this whole thing get to her. But the backhanded way Metin's father intimated he hadn't approved of Alicia and Metin's marriage still niggled at her. "Did you guys.... I mean, did you not like Alicia? I mean, not that it matters now."

Timur frowned and faced her, his expression dark. She allowed herself a split second to admire the perfection of the man. He was as handsome as his younger brother, which was saying something since Metin Sevim deserved his "hottest guy on the soccer pitch" accolades—at least she supposed he used to. "It wasn't that we didn't like her. It was more a concern about Metin." He flapped his hand, seeming at a loss for words. "He gets so attached so quickly, without thinking, usually." The man stared at her, and her heart pounded. "He is our parents' favorite, the youngest, the famous football golden boy. But he's always been emotionally immature. We figured Alicia for another in a long string of women. Different, yes, because she played his game, but we honestly thought it was, um, like a fad for him. That he would outgrow the whole thing. I'm sorry. I'm not making this sound very good."

The fury Mel had sustained for so long, a comfortable, almost easy chair-like thing, faded ever so slightly. She'd felt the same way about Metin—that he had been a fling, something Alicia had latched onto for some strange reason and would grow out of, hence her own aggravation about the pregnancy and her eagerness to rid her sister of the excuse to stay with him.

She put her hands on her thighs, which trembled slightly. "I understand. I know how you felt. But I guess they fooled us all."

"Something like that." Timur grabbed her arm, startling her out of a haze. "Help us get him back. Please. You and he clashed from the start, but at this point, we figured he'd emerge from hiding just to, I don't know, fight with you or something. You're the last person on earth he would expect, maybe. And perhaps the one he'll listen to and stop all this... this... shit."

A small corner of her heart flexed, like an atrophied muscle, at the sight of how upset the man was, at the thought of losing his little brother to the sort of heartbreak that none of them could truly fathom. She put out a shaky hand to touch his face. He clutched it, hung on as if she were the last life preserver on the Titanic.

The intensity of his gaze brought ever-hovering tears to the surface. He looked so much like an older version of the very man she had harbored such hatred for in the last few years. She had zero business here, in their country, in a teeming foreign city, making this intervention or whatever the hell it was. She wanted to go home.

"Thank you for coming here Melanie and for agreeing to help us, to help him. I know how you feel about him, and sometimes I understand it. I'm his older brother and I resented the shit out of him from the minute he was born and my mother decided he was the chosen one, you know?" He let go of her hand, taking the steering wheel in a death grip again.

Mel smiled. "We're more simpatico than you might think," she said under her breath. Then she got out without another word and wiped the moisture from her forehead. Istanbul in September felt like the inside of an oven, with extra car exhaust piped in to provide atmosphere.

Approaching the building with a pounding heart, she flashed the key card to the doorman and entered the giant elevator. She slid the card into the slot to allow her access to the upper floors. The lift shot silently upward way too fast.

When it stopped, she stood, frozen once more. She'd spent so much energy blocking anything and everything about her sister's husband from her brain that it felt odd to acknowledge she wasn't sure she'd know him if she saw him. Every single time she'd laid eyes on him, there had been some sort of conflict, some way that she, Mel, ended up playing bitchy older sister. She had absolutely no idea what she would do when and if she did lay eyes on him.

The elevator doors slid open, revealing a tall, barely dressed woman was screeching at the top of her lungs, interspersed with bouts of kicking and beating on a dark wood door.. Mel noted the number on it was the same one she'd been told to open with the key she held in her sweat-slick palm.

She approached the woman having some sort of fit, watching as she pulled at her long hair, sobbed and called Metin's name.

The woman reeked of booze, cigarettes, and the distinct underlay of sex. She whipped around fast, gibbering in Turkish, her face beautiful but tear-streaked. Amused and angry at the same time, Mel held up her hands, unsure how to progress, worried that the crazy bitch would launch herself at her and start ripping out her eyes.

"English?" she asked.

"Who the fuck are you?" the woman spit out with only a slight accent. "How do you have a key? Metin! Metin! Goddamn you, son of a pig fucker," she screamed and kicked at the door some more, then slid down the wall, crying.

Even as she had to admire the insult, Mel ignored her. But as soon as she inserted the card into the slot, the crazy woman pushed past her into the condo. Shaking her head, Mel stood and took in the chaos that bordered on squalor of the expansive space. She touched the toe of her shoe to the pile of clothing nearest her and wrinkled her nose at the stacks of plates and glasses and empty bottles on the glass table in front of the leather couch.

She made her way into the kitchen, shoved a pile of mail to the floor and took a seat at the table, trying to shrink inside her clothing. The view out of the floor-to-ceiling windows caught her eye. Giant barges moved up and down the Bosporus, cars buzzed across multiple bridges between Europe and Asia, all in complete silence, hypnotizing her.

Nearly thirty minutes went by before she heard anything else, and by that time she'd strolled around the living room, noting the distinct lack of photos anywhere. There were, however, plenty of dirty clothes, dishes, food containers, empty bottles of booze, soda, juice, and at least one mirror dusted with white powder. When she finally identified the half a dozen used condoms all over the place, she wanted to retch or punch the dickhead right in his stupid face.

The kitchen was no better. There were stains all over the marble tile floor and a horrific stench that could only be weeks-old garbage combined with sour milk emanating from an under-counter garbage pail. Using a pair of tongs she found in a drawer, she picked what appeared to be a pair of men's underwear off the counter and tossed them to the floor. Then she saw a single photo—one of Metin, Alicia, and Ayden at the boy's first birthday party. Numb from jetlag and her own conflict about being here, she stared into the eyes of her dead sister and nephew.

A yell of something that could be fury or delight made her drop the framed picture, shattering the glass covering it. Mel cursed as a shard of it went through the pad of her finger when she tried to clean it up while ignoring the sloppy kissing noises behind her.

"Metin...," the girl whined then launched into a string of slurred-sounding Turkish.

Mel got to her feet, holding the photo, determined to take it and hightail the hell out of the place. Metin was in fine hands. She had no responsibility to or for him. Not if he treated himself and his expensive condo like this. Something dark loomed in her, frightened at being in such proximity to him again. The need to escape grew so strong it pounded against her ribcage like a drumbeat.

When she heard his voice, tears filled her eyes at the ghostly echoes of memory his rumbling cadence evoked. He rounded the corner into the kitchen and stopped, mid-sentence, his mouth hanging open at the sight of her. She stood straighter, attempting to gather a cloak of self-righteousness around herself. But she was shocked to see how thin he was, a clichéd shadow of himself. Her pulse raced, worry etching a small track in her brain. She gave herself a mental shake and tried to find words. There were none.

"Sorry," she muttered, starting to move past him. "I shouldn't have come here. Carry on with your party." She gestured around to the disgusting mess that comprised his life now.

He grabbed her arm, his grip tight. Mel's face flushed, noting the mask of pure agony on his face.

"Metin? Who is this?" Crazy slut woman inserted herself between them, wrapping her arms around his neck and forcing him to let go of

Mel's arm. His face morphed into something else, something Mel had never seen and didn't like.

"I told you," he growled in English. "Get the hell out of here and don't come back."

He peeled her off of him like a banana skin and marched her across the room. She tried to stay barnacled, but he pushed her into the hall and slammed the door in her face. Mel froze, watching it, observing his bare, dark-skinned shoulders until he whipped around and pinned her with a look so full of hate she sucked in a breath and took a step back from him.

"And you," he spit out, crossing his arms. "What in the name of all that's holy brings you here?"

She stammered, gulped, searching for any sort of logical answer to a perfectly good question. Why was she there, in Istanbul, thousands of miles from her home, family, and business trying to help him? She let the familiar Metin-inspired rage cloud the edges of her vision.

"Well?" he demanded, moving closer and forcing her farther back until her butt hit the wall. "Seen enough yet?" He gestured around. "The ruination of a star. The fall of football's great one. The downward spiral of a man devastated by loss. I'm sure that you love seeing me like this."

His dark eyes flashed with a mix of anger and misery. He continued moving toward her until they were inches apart, and she stood face-to-face, literally, with the man she hated so deeply she could taste it—a scary, coppery, metallic thing she'd once excused as righteous anger on behalf of her now dead sister. She tried to calm her racing pulse, while rage, jetlag and a surging sense of dismay filled her entire being, making her want to lie down and sleep for a week. The sight of him wallowing like this, his once-athletic frame scrawny, his hair too long and his skin sallow was affecting her and not in the way she wanted it to. When she dug at the feeling that was blooming in her chest, she realized it was pity.

"All this—it must make you very happy. Are you? Happy now?" He bit the words off, flung them at her, making her blink in the face of them.

She forced her gaze away. He propped his hands on either side of her head. "Go ahead and look at me, Melanie." His lips and tongue caressed her name, drawing out the syllables in a sing-song way she didn't remember from any other time he'd used it. She shook her head to clear the encroaching scramble of emotions that included a tiny corner of something she identified as lust, made a mental note to get herself laid, then shoved him aside. The fact that he was easy to push away only reinforced the facts in front of her face—he was, indeed, a different man, a changed man, a man reduced to something pitiable.

"Go get a shower while I clean this place up. It's the least I can do before I leave."

Her hands shook so badly when she tried to turn on the kitchen faucet, she had to stop and clench them together a few seconds. By the time she had the dishwasher loaded and the bulk of the kitchen and dining areas tidy and had located a vacuum cleaner, he'd emerged from the bathroom wearing a pair of shorts and a black t-shirt. His hair was wet, and his eyes downcast, reminding her of a little boy presenting himself for punishment after putting a frog in his brother's bed or something equally ridiculous.

"Here." She thrust the vacuum at him. "Do this while I..."

She stared down at the hand he'd put on her arm. It had come from nowhere and was burning her skin in a way she had no explanation for. "I'm sorry," he muttered, letting her go in the face of her glare.

She headed for the living room, her ears buzzing and her face so hot she knew she must be beet red. After tossing a bunch of clothes into the washing machine and hoping she'd turned the thing on correctly, she found him collecting all the old take out cartons and other trash. His general demeanor was one of utter defeat.

"Do you have tea? Of course you do," she asked and answered herself before marching into the now pristine kitchen, seeking something to do with her hands.

She filled and turned on the electric kettle and rustled around in the many cabinets for cups. She didn't trust herself to prepare traditional Turkish tea properly and hoped there were bags or something somewhere. "Where in the hell do you keep the—oh," she yelped when she felt a hand on her shoulder. "Jesus, don't sneak up on a girl like that."

She turned to face him. He was holding out a jar of loose tea and two cup-sized strainers. "Thanks," she said, taking them and putting them to use while he stood nearby, making her nervous. She stared at the kettle, willing it to hurry up, keeping her back to him since she didn't trust herself or what crazy thing she might do if she turned around again.

What in heaven's name was wrong with her? She despised the man lurking near her left shoulder. But damn if something about him, something in his broken posture, sad face, and big brown eyes were making her want to, what? Cuddle him? Wow. She really did have jet lag.

"Don't," she said when she sensed him move closer, then had to bite back a groan of embarrassment when she realized he was moving past her to the fridge. "You don't have any cream. I checked already. You don't have much of anything, really."

She busied herself with the tea, gnawing on the inside of her cheek so hard she was going to regret it later. Once each tea ball was steeping inside its own mug, she carried them to the table she'd cleaned off, determined to get the hell out of here, fast. He was there already, sitting like a schoolboy with his hands folded in front of him. There was a small box in the middle of the table, something he must have retrieved from the mostly empty fridge or freezer. She set the mugs down and felt a tear slide down her cheek when she realized it was a box of Alicia's favorite strawberry candies.

She swiped at her face, not willing to let him see her emotions, opened the box and took one out. She used to hate the damn things, had no idea why Alicia loved them so much, but had developed a taste for them in the last couple of years. "Nice touch," she said, before popping it into her mouth. He nodded and pulled his cup closer, wrapping both hands around its warmth. She sat, swallowed the candy, and yanked her tea ball out of the mug before taking a sip, scalding the entire inside of her mouth in the process. "Shit, shit, ow," she yelped as she headed for the sink.

When she turned around, Metin was there, holding out an ice cube. He wasn't smiling. But he did look somewhat amused at her discomfort. The sight of that slight smirk comforted her, put things back in balance, somehow. She took the cube, frowned at him and stuck it in her mouth. He held out his hand. She stared at it, confused.

"Truce?" he said, his voice hoarse.

"Sure, fine, truce, whatever." She shook his hand. A mistake, since she had to yank her palm away from his, horrified by the shock of their contact and what it was doing to her brain.

"I'm sorry, Metin. I'm so...so...s-s-s-" Her entire body was shaking. After a few seconds of hesitation, she leaned toward him until he held out his arms. She fell into him like a ton of bricks, sending him stumbling backwards until they hit the counter, her hands twisted in the back of his shirt, her face pressed into his neck. At one point, she realized that she was being held by the man she'd been blaming for her sister's death for the past two years. But the relief of allowing herself to cry overshadowed her horror at her current position. She let the tears fall, especially once she realized that he was crying along with her.

Chapter Four

The fog surrounding Metin's soul for the last months remained fixed firmly in place. He hurt all over, every day. Not one molecule of him didn't pulse with raw agony twenty-four-seven. His chest ached, head pounded, stomach refused to accept food.

His life had ended when he walked out of that hospital in Michigan, leaving behind his heart and soul and only shot at true happiness. All that was left to him was drinking, fucking, sleeping, and waking up to begin again—a merry-go-round of uselessness. He felt scraped out, a husk that he re-filled with booze, women, and strange beds.

In the months since his family's destruction, he'd spent something like a sum total of thirty minutes sober. Rendered a lightweight from years of strict self-discipline—no alcohol during La Liga's season and certainly none if there were World Cup qualifiers or during the once-every-four-years that he played with his own Turkish national team. He certainly was one no more.

His agent had done his level best to get Metin out of Turkey and back to Madrid once training began. The club gave him plenty of leeway, considering circumstances and his star status. And he'd thanked them by showing up hung over, three weeks later than everyone else, woefully out of shape, and furious at the world. His anger manifested itself within minutes of a friendly—read: low contact—scrimmage.

The coach had to run out onto the field himself and practically sit on Metin to get him to calm down, while his teammates cursed and held hands over broken noses, busted lips, and, in one case, a fractured toe. He barely remembered a moment of it, other than the red-tinged anger that he'd exorcised by beating the living shit out of the men opposite him on the field, never mind they were on his team.

If he were honest, he hardly remembered anything from those first six or seven months. Orgasmic over the drama, the foreign press shoved its way into his face and life even more, catching him out in the wee hours draped over this or that random starlet, drunk, and on occasion, high. After a while they lost interest, moving on to the next story, but he could be assured that if he were screwing up in public, it would be photographed.

Real Madrid put up with it a lot longer than some clubs might have. But he was Metin Sevim, wonder-boy player, superstar forward, the ballet master of the pitch, blah blah blah. And fans paid good money to see him play. But it seemed the harder they tried to get him to clean up and fly straight, the more crooked he went, thumbing his nose at their interest in him as a player or even as a human being.

The problem was, he could give a fuck about soccer any more.

Halfway through the fall season, Madrid traded him down to Valencia, where he got into a giant brawl with a ref, nearly breaking the guy's arm in a fit of rage before puking on the sidelines. That photo greased the skids of soccer gossip headlines for weeks, and got him booted to a place of honor on the bench for the rest of the season, when he bothered to show up for the games. Finally, he ended up playing in Turkey, on one of the premiere Istanbul-based teams, as a bit of a show pony. His homeland treated him with a little more respect, at least at first. They understood his grief and seemed willing to let him wallow in it.

Once there, he'd felt justified, appreciated by his own people. Until he showed up roaring drunk to a game against their arch, cross-town rival. That pretty much shoved what remained of his career all the way down into the toilet and given it a firm flush. Leaving him here, in an over-priced condo with absolutely nothing to do but cry himself to sleep when memories would not be drowned in alcohol or between the thighs of yet another nameless woman.

After beating up anyone who came to drag him out of his hole, including his brothers, everyone left him alone. He had no patience for being saved. There was nothing in him worth saving. He wanted to die. Many a night, leaning into the wind that whipped across the large balcony of his condo, he'd been on the verge of taking care of that death wish himself.

The sight of Alicia's sister Melanie here in his sink hole of a condo shoved open the booze-soaked, heavy doors slammed over what was left of his heart, leaving it exposed, raw, and bleeding again. He'd been briefly tempted to kiss her, to drag her to his bed, and he'd bet money she'd go. They were both broken beyond repair. Why not shove them both over the edge, in what would at least be a temporarily pleasant way? But something about the way she stared at him as he loomed over her, ready to jump in with both feet and stomp around a while, made him pause, then stop.

Thank god.

She hated him. Why exacerbate that? But she was also the one thing he had that tied him to the life he'd loved. He was left shivering and sweaty with remorse, a hangover, and the never-absent agony of his loss as he watched her march into the kitchen and start clanking around after telling him to go take a shower. His head cleared at the firm sound of her voice. Yes, a shower. That would help.

When he came back into the kitchen, his head pounding and his guts churning, she shoved the vacuum cleaner into his hands. He stared at it a few minutes, dumbfounded. Until he recalled that the cleaning service his mother had sent quit in disgust a month ago and he hadn't done anything about it since. After fiddling with the thing for a few minutes to figure out how to turn it on, he passed it over the carpets and hardwood. It was soothing to focus on it and not his own misery.

He finished, wrapped the cord around the hooks on the back of it, then tried to recall where it went. After depositing it in the laundry room, where both machines were going, thanks to Melanie's efforts, he returned to the kitchen. Seeking more orders of where to go, what to do, how to distract himself in a way that didn't involve drinking, or grabbing the gorgeous woman messing around with the tea kettle and tossing her on the bed.

He shook his head.

Stop it, man. That is just... sick. She's your dead wife's sister and would probably bite your dick off if you tried to get anywhere near her. Never mind, you'd prove her original point about him—that he was a no-good, full-of-himself, playboy. Nope. He wouldn't give her that satisfaction.

He handed her tea leaves that were probably stale, plus the strainers. Then, being the well-trained host that he was, went to the freezer to find something to eat with their tea. His heart broke all over again at the sight of the small See's Candies box, but he grabbed it and tossed it down on the table before slumping into a seat.

His ears were ringing again, a newly familiar sensation which blocked out almost everything around him. A mug of fragrant tea was set in front of him. He wrapped both his hands around it, willing some warmth into his extremities. When Melanie cursed and ran to the sink, he got up, took an ice cube from the freezer, and handed it to her, more or less on autopilot. Alicia used to burn her mouth on her tea all the time. It figured that her sister would, too.

But at that moment, the entirety of his loss hit him square in the chest, making it hard to breathe, making him wish he were dead. Melanie was staring at the now melting ice cube in his hand as if he were asking her to grab a venomous snake. A small noise escaped her lips, confusing him until he took a good look at her. She was shaking as if having a seizure. Familiar with this now, after two years' worth of suffering himself, he reached for her. Her full-body tremors absorbed into him, calming him. He stumbled backwards but held onto her, knowing this was what she needed, even as he realized how odd it was that he'd be the one to provide her with emotional support.

His own tears flowed along with hers. He wasn't sure how long they stood, his back against the kitchen counter, crying along with his dead wife's angry sister. Finally, she broke away, sniffled, and swiped at her eyes.

"I'm here to bring you to America. To coach some new team. Did my tactic work?" She raised an eyebrow at him. But the fresh tear that slid down her cheek belied her nonchalance.

Fury gripped him. That, combined with surprised horror at her lame attempt at a joke, made him want to put his fist through the wall. His head pounded. His heart ached. He ran a hand down his face, drank some water, and attempted to process what was happening.

"You should go, Melanie. I'm not worth the effort." He didn't recognize the sound of his own voice.

The familiar harshness of her laughter made him shiver. God, he had hated her and her need to keep Alicia under her thumb. Opening his eyes, he met her glare—also something he remembered—which relaxed him in a perverse way.

"No, I think you and I need to sit and have an adult conversation. I don't give two shits about you, but I've been asked to consider my sister's legacy. So I'm here to tell you that you are dishonoring her with your behavior." She crossed her arms. Metin ground his teeth and grabbed the photo of his dead family that she'd left on the island, clutching it close to his chest like a shield.

"I'm... it's... you know what? Fuck you."

"Ah, ah, ah, now watch what you say there, soccer boy. You don't want to make idle threats." She held up a trembling hand.

Taking a deep breath, he stuck his hands on his hips. "I can't imagine what makes you think I would come to America and coach a team of has-beens. Especially if it means being anywhere near you." He had to concentrate on keeping his expression angry. Because at that precise moment, he wasn't sure if his desire not to be anywhere near her had more to do with a sudden desire to kiss her angry, pursed lips.

Oh damn. I'm losing it.

She drew herself up to her full height. He had to avoid gawking at her angular beauty. What he had once taken for hard lines were more like lean, appealing curves. He curled his hands into fists, prepared to punch himself in the face for even pondering touching, much less kissing her. Because that's exactly what he was doing, and he knew this particular pondering moment would come back to haunt him.

To his surprise, her expression softened, and she slumped, as if defeated. "Let's sit a minute, drink some tea so I can report to your desperate family that you are indeed alive and still as much of an asshole as I remembered." She smiled then, and for some reason, his knees gave out. He was standing one second, crumpled to the floor the next, cradling the photo of his family, rocking, keening, making the most obnoxious noises.

And Mel was there, on the floor with him. Her arms were around him and he buried his face in her neck. The tears he'd already shed would fill a hundred oceans, but still they came, salty, unwelcome, and painful, ripping at his chest, burning their way down his raw face.

He clung to her and didn't know where his tears ended and hers began. "I'm sorry. I'm so sorry. I'm...." He sucked in a breath, unwilling to let her go. "I want to die."

"Shh...." She rocked with him. "You aren't going to die. She would never forgive me if I let that happen."

A surge of hysteria caught in his throat, frightening him. But she held him close, and for the first time in nearly two years, he didn't feel utterly alone.

Chapter Five

She knew, even as she found herself trapped in its grip, that the nightmare had returned. The heavy drawer slid open, the sheet pulled away, and there lay her beautiful, perfect nephew, his skull crushed almost beyond recognition, his sweet voice silenced forever in the screech of metal and blood.

She reached for him. But Metin was there, yelling and trying to drag the boy into his arms. Hands pulled her away, forced her down into a chair to watch her brother-in-law fly apart at the seams. Her father remained stoic. And for the most part, so did she, remaining strong in the face of Metin's breakdown.

She thrashed around, forcing herself awake. Something heavy held her down, and she gasped, trying to sit up, terrified, until she realized Metin's arm draped over her chest while he snored softly next to her. They must have fallen asleep on his couch after she conjured up some semblance of a meal out of his fridge contents, forced him to eat it, and held him off from the wine bottle he wanted to open.

"Nope. I think you've had enough booze to last several lifetimes."

He'd scowled, but set it aside, sipping the water she put in front of him, his silence thick with unhappiness. She had teenage boys, so that was nothing new to her. But there was something else now, something buzzing and irritating and unfamiliar between them. And once she outed that sensation as capital L Lust and for the man she'd harbored such visceral hate over for so long, she was mortified. But they'd eaten the meal in silence, watched something random on the giant television that she didn't register. He'd cleaned the dishes in the newly tidy kitchen while she dozed.

"Scoot over," he said, when he returned holding a soft blanket. She scooted, accepted the blanket, realizing that he meant for them to be under it together a little too late, then surrendered to the siren call of sleep.

Now, in the sweaty aftermath of the dream, she struggled out from under his arm, escaped to a nearby leather chair, and watched him. The dark-olive hue of his skin, the black scruff of beard, his still-broad shoulders and arms mesmerized her. Giving herself a firm, inner lecture, she got up, located a clean towel and availed herself of the shower in his massive bathroom.

Cranking the water all the way hot, she swayed under the stream, letting it beat the shame out of her at how badly she wanted to walk in there and... and... what? Be connected to a man she had no business thinking about in any way, much less a sexual one. She took a deep breath, relishing the smell of the soap—sandalwood with a hint of citrus. She used it all over her body. After a near solid hour, she emerged, pink-skinned and exhausted.

"Whoa!" she yelped, nearly plowing right into Metin. He'd positioned himself in the doorway, arms crossed, a smile playing at his lips. "You scared me." She moved away, clutching the towel, embarrassed and pissed at the same time. "Excuse me," she muttered, sliding past him.

He touched her bare shoulder. "Is it weird that I like having you here?"

She shivered, but stepped well away from him.

This is not happening. She was an adult woman with nearly-grown boys, and she had to get the hell away from this guy. Damn man was a walking flesh-bag of testosterone. He was... her dead sister's husband.

Good god, Melanie, get a grip

"No. Yes. I don't know." She sighed. "Let me get dressed and we'll talk."

He leaned against the wall, eyes trained up at the ceiling. "I'm sorry, Melanie."

The sound of her name crossing his lips sent a fresh bolt of lust flaming down her spine. She sucked in a breath, felt on the verge of potentially making the worst choice of her life. "For what?" The hoarseness of her voice betrayed her. His eyes darkened but he kept his distance.

"For all of it. For taking your sister away from her family. For fighting with her that Christmas. For..."

She held up a shaking hand. "Enough. I get it. It's...fine." She dropped her hand and clutched the towel closer, feeling like some kind of an old lady, embarrassed about her bare skin showing.

"I need to confess something," she said, leaning against the wall opposite him.

"I'm listening."

She shook her head to clear it of the clear vision of her launching herself across the hallway at him, tackling him to the ground, kissing those full lips. She shivered.

"Are you cold?" He reached past her and produced a silky-looking robe.

"No, god damn you. Stop being...nice." She sniffled and took the robe anyway. "Turn around."

He turned and she slid her arms into the robe, tied the belt tight and let the towel drop to the floor. Feeling a bit more in control of herself, she ran her fingers through her wet hair and took a deep breath. "Okay. You can look at me now."

He smiled when he faced her, which did nothing to quell the alarming rush of desire that had been smoldering for the last few hours. "So..." he said.

"So...what?" She was back to being the stuttering, horny old lady and she hated it. But damn her if she couldn't practically feel his skin under her fingers.

"Your confession?"

"Oh, right. Um...yeah." She tugged the robe's belt even tighter. "So, the thing is, I was jealous."

He snorted. "Oh, okay. Tell me something I didn't already know."

Fury flamed in her chest so she grabbed onto it, grateful for something other than the hovering fog of annoying lust. "Listen, asshole. It wasn't you, specifically. It was the fact that Alicia found something so, I don't know, real but at the same time a kind of a fairy tale with you."

He took a single step toward her, closing the gap between them. She tried to step back from him but her butt hit the wall. When he touched her cheek, she flinched, then leaned into his hand. "I know that's hard for you to admit," he said, his voice soft.

"Please, just, don't." She moved to the side, out of his reach, grasping at the robe, trying to cover herself to hide how flushed she'd gotten at his touch. "It's not right."

He sighed and ran his hand down his face. "I know. I'm sorry."

"I'm going to get dressed," she said, easing past him. "I'll meet you in the kitchen."

She slammed the door shut to the bedroom where she'd left her clothes. But they smelled sour, like she'd flown a zillion miles and sweated the entire time. Tears burned her eyes. Always the damned tears. She swiped at them and flopped onto the bed, holding her smelly, nasty clothes and wondering what in the hell she'd gotten herself into. She'd walked into this building determined to make an effort to convince a man she despised to get his act together for her dead sister's and nephew's sakes. And now it was all she could do to not run out of the room and jump his stupid—sexy—bones.

Ugh. She was mental.

"I need to go home," she said out loud, standing up and stripping off the robe that smelled like Metin's soap, determined to get a grip on her libido and get the hell on a plane pointed to Michigan, and fast. A soft knock on the door made her yelp out loud, then clap a hand over her mouth, embarrassed. "What?" She kept her voice in the Melanie-is-a-total-bitch range lest he get any ideas.

"There are some clothes in the drawers, on the far wall, if you want something clean," Metin said.

"How do you have...oh. Never mind." She pulled open the drawers, yanked out a pair of shorts and a tee shirt, then threw them onto the floor and stomped over the closet. Sure enough, it was chock full of dresses, blouses, skirts, purses, belts—all of it belonging to her sister. Her throat closed up, but she muscled past it. She had to get the hell out of here.

She yanked a soft-looking, black, t-shirt style dress off a hanger, decided against wearing panties, put on her bra and pulled the dress on in a fit of batting emotions. Muttering under her breath about her own lameness, she dragged her fingers through her hair, then, knowing what she'd find, she opened a drawer in the adjacent bathroom. It was overflowing with ponytail holders, clips, and headbands. She stared at them for exactly ten seconds, then grabbed one and slammed the drawer shut.

"Melanie?"

She shut her eyes at the fresh rush of longing. Je-sus but she needed to go home and find a boyfriend or a man friend or a friend with benefits. Something, anything, to deny the near overwhelming need for a man's hands on her body that was coursing through her right now. Hair sorted, clothes on, she stuck her feet back into her sandals and stuffed her panties into the pocket in the dress. Leave it to her sister to find a perfect dress that had pockets.

She smiled at the thought of Alicia, which was a departure for her—normally any thoughts of her brought tears and rage. "Oh...crap." Mel's knees wobbled. She sat on the edge of the bed, eyes clenched shut. What was happening to her? How in god's name was she in this place, thinking these thoughts?

"Fuck," she spat out and got to her feet. Men were the bane of her existence. She'd never lacked for dates or attention but her ex-husband had fucking ruined her. And that's why she'd been so damn jealous of

Alicia and her hot soccer man and their perfect life with a closets full of dresses with god damned "Pockets!" She clapped a hand over her lips again, realizing she'd blurted the word out loud.

"You all right in there?"

"Yes. Sorry. I'm..." Screw it, she thought, throwing the door open and marching back into the living room. "I'm leaving."

Metin looked up at her, his expression somewhere between confused, hurt, and grateful. He rose to his feet. She busied herself making sure she had her phone, her bag, her wits about her. "So, are you coming? Back home, I mean. What am I supposed to tell these soccer people?"

"I'll call them," he said, his shoulders slumped. Mel had to dig her fingernails into her palm to keep from rushing to him, pulling him close, feeling his strong body...

She squared her shoulders. "Okay then. Good. Great. I wish you, um, nothing but the best."

He watched her walk to the door. She had it halfway open when she sensed him close again, too close. It took everything she had in her not to turn to him, to acknowledge and purge the massive thing that had risen its horny head between them. But she stepped into the hallway and walked to the elevator without a word. He was still standing in the condo doorway when she turned to face him once she got into the elevator.

He raised a hand in farewell. She raised hers. And the doors slid shut.

• • • •

METIN SAT WITH HIS feet propped up on the balcony banister, dressed in shorts and nothing more, staring out into the purple darkness over his hometown. He sipped water and tried not to give into the urge to open a bourbon bottle and drink the whole thing. Warm wind caressed his skin.

He ran a hand down his chest, feeling how small it had gotten, how weak he'd become. He groaned and leaned over his knees, trying not to be sick.

This is what rock-fucking-bottom looks like. Take a long, hard gander at it because you own this now. This place where you are so pitiful you actually thought about kissing her, fucking her, holding her close—Melanie, your dead wife's sister..

But he was still thinking about it, wondering if he should have done something before she walked out the door. God help him and curse him straight to hell. He jumped to his feet, put his hand on the railing, and let the wind prop him up. How many times had he been in that very spot, ready to count to three and leap over the side, to sail down in a swan dive of relief, to leave all the shit behind him? His career was ruined. Everything he loved had been taken from him and why? What had he done? The night mocked him with its silence, like it had been since the moment he had kissed his beloved good-bye.

And now?

He turned, facing away from the railing, pondering how much he'd complicated everything by allowing that he'd loved it when she'd held him, when he'd held her, when they'd given into their grief together. The universe was conspiring against him now. Putting Alicia's once-bitchy sister in his path. If he had a nickel for every time he and Alicia had argued about her, he'd be even richer.

On autopilot, he made a carafe of French press coffee, poured a cup and sat, holding two business cards she'd left on the counter. One for Rafael Inez, the other for Jack Gordon, both emblazoned with some kind of poker chip, playing card combined emblem, and the words, BlackJack Gentlemen. The Soccer Team of Detroit.

Emotions bombarded him from all directions—anger, defensiveness, remorse, guilt, sadness—then circled back to anger again. He picked up the cards, still calling down all manner of curses on Melanie for coming here. But if she showed up again, right then, he'd be so relieved, he'd fall at her feet and beg her forgiveness. He knew himself well enough that he didn't do "alone" well at all, hence the string of various women he'd run through since his wife and son's horrible accident.

But the loneliness he felt right then, deep in his gut, had nothing whatsoever to do with needing a female body near his. That he could make one phone call and procure. No, he required someone to talk to over coffee, argue with, laugh with, get mad at and make up. He may very well want the forbidden fruit of the older sister. He might want her for some of the wrong reasons, but so many more of them were right. She represented so much he missed about his life, in an utterly bizarre way, but still...

He grabbed his phone, fingers poised, ready to dial his house and tell his mother to send Melanie back over when she showed up. Instead, he picked up Rafael's card and dialed that number, taking a long, deep breath and along with it, a small step out of the hellish emotional prison he'd inhabited for so long.

Chapter Six

Mel dropped her bag on the counter and repressed the urge to burst into tears at the sight of the demolished kitchen when she got home from a long day at the restaurant. That, or shake Zach until his teeth rattled. Neither option was viable. Nor would they do any good. Ever since she'd returned from Turkey, her mind a whirlwind of confusion, it seemed her older son was going further and further out of his way to vex her. She'd discovered long ago that teenage boys were vexatious creatures under the best of circumstances. But damn if the kid didn't seem determined to write a whole new chapter in the "how to be a pissed off teenager" book.

"Zachary!" She tried to not let her voice betray how close she was to furious tears. Pissed off teenaged boys sensed weakness like a predator sensed prey. Tanner rushed into the kitchen to give her a hug which she accepted, eyes closed, fatigue looming. When she walked into the family room, she found Zach slung across a chair, eyes on his phone by way of ignoring her.

"Zach!" the younger boy yelled at his brother. "Come clean the kitchen. You said you would."

"Whatever."

Mel bit the inside of her cheek, counted to twenty, then stood between her oldest son and the television which he was also ignoring. "Zach, did you ever hear from a guy named Rafe who was going to help you with your scholarship stuff?" She forced her voice to remain level.

"Yeah." He grunted, not looking up from his phone.

"And?" She shifted to the side, snagged the remote, and clicked the TV off.

"Watching that," he said with a classic eye roll.

"Tell me how it's going then." She sat across from him, determined to keep her own temper under control, to remain the adult in the room. "Not the tv show, the recruiting stuff."

43

Heavy sigh, followed by, "he's got some people coming to film me so I have new clips to send or something... and he knows the coaches at State and Purdue and Georgia Tech."

Unable to stop herself, she snagged the kid's phone so he would be forced to look at her.

"Hey!"

"Hey yourself. Focus on me for ten seconds, please. Surely this is a tad more important than Snap Doodles or Face Toks or whatever the hell."

Tanner giggled. Zach frowned at him, but she saw his lips curl up into a smile before he focused on her.

"Rafe says I've got a decent shot at a scholarship at a few places."

Mel took a slow breath. "Good. I'm glad to hear it. Now get up off your ass and clean the kitchen while I take a shower. Then I'll make us pancakes for dinner." She tossed his phone back in his lap.

"Gotta make some Doodle Toks," Tanner said, dropping onto the couch and turning the television back on.

"Yeah, then a few Insta Chats," Zach said, making Tanner giggle again.

She smiled at the quick flash of happiness on Zach's face, reminding her of the little boy he'd been—a handful, to be sure, but hers nonetheless. Her sons kept razzing each other, yelling from room to room while Zach worked in the kitchen. So she headed up the steps to her bathroom, eager for a few minutes not spent teaching new servers how to serve or her sons how to clean up after themselves.

The water hit her skin, washing away the day's long, hot painfulness. She'd had to fire a couple of her employees who were popular amongst the staff but who'd gotten so many complaints from customers she had no choice. Mel loved her business but hated being the boss sometimes and wished she had a friend or two to unwind with who didn't hate her guts because—or in spite of the fact that—she signed their paychecks. And they were real paychecks, too. She paid a living wage, and let her staff keep tips. She knew it was risky but it had kept Ayden's from being too much of a revolving door, employee-wise.

As she passed her hands down her body, a shiver of memory made her grip the tiled walls to keep from dropping to her knees. Metin had sent her an email that week. She'd spent a lot of energy ignoring the message, afraid of her own response to the sight of his name. That whole encounter in Istanbul had been so surreal, she still wondered what might have happened if either of them had taken a step towards what seemed inevitable—at least at the time. Now that she had some time and physical distance from it, it had retreated to the corners of her psyche, thank goodness.

Men were off her radar, permanently. The thing with Metin had been am emotional connection and one that had surprised her, but nothing more than two people desperate to dispel some demons of memory. Their dual crying jags had been cathartic. They'd comforted each other, nothing more or less. And now, she had to ignore him, even if he did move to Michigan. But he was reaching out to her for some reason, if that damn message sitting in her inbox was any indication.

She slipped into clean jeans and a T-shirt and sat in her favorite squishy leather chair, staring at her lap top resting on a small table, open to her email. Finally she reached out, hovering over the delete button. "Just read the thing. It's not gonna bite you," she berated herself as she opened the email sent four days prior.

Dear Melanie,

I need you to know that I'm sincerely sorry for the scene at Alicia and Ayden's funeral. I wanted to say this to your face, but your exit was so fast I didn't get a chance.

I also want to apologize for some of the things I assumed about you. I am the product of a chauvinistic culture, and one that is brutally hypocritical as well. We expect our women to be beautiful, perfect creatures to the eye, pliable and soft underneath, and when we come up against one who is as hard as nails under her lovely surface... sometimes we act in ways that shame us. I did that to you for years, without really understanding it. Your sister was that way, too, in her way. Believe it or not, we clashed on many things, but because I loved her so much, I was evolving, let's say, thanks to her.

I have been in touch with the team in Detroit and will be in Michigan on Friday, staying through until the next Thursday to tour their facility and meet the players they have in place already. I doubt that I will take the job, however. I don't know if I can coach, and I'm shocked that they seem to think that I can.

You must know that if you hadn't shown up here that day, I don't know where I'd be right now. However you feel about me, please know that you may have saved my life. I've spent the last few weeks getting back in shape, detoxing from booze, and generally attempting to get through each day not so angry or despairing.

Yours,

Metin (aka the soccer-playing asshole)

Mel frowned, startled at the sound of Zach clearing his throat from behind her. "Hey, uh, Mom?"

She shook her head, unable to focus, her eyes locked on her small screen.

"There's someone at the door...." She turned to him, her skin flushing at the realization of what was happening right now. Zach's face remained blank, but his eyes blazed with something she didn't understand.

Her heart pounded as she glanced back at the email message.

Friday. As in today.

• • • •

METIN CLIMBED OUT OF the rental car and walked up the sidewalk to Melanie's tidy bungalow, a smile fixed on his face. He'd come here first on purpose, hoping to clear the air with her in person. She'd not responded to his email, which he didn't take as a good sign.

But he needed her to know how much she'd helped him, that he was attempting to move on with his life, and that he'd leave her alone once he got this off his chest.

A tall young man answered the door. Metin's smile widened at the sight of him. The boy's frown deepened in response.

"Hi Zach, you have certainly grown. Um, do you remember me?" The kid didn't move or blink. He simply stood, blocking the doorway. "Metin?" He stuck out a hand.

"Yeah, I remember you. Why are you here?"

"I'm, uh...." He was at a sudden loss for words. His head pounded. He wanted a drink, to go home, to avoid this whole scene at all costs. But he squared his shoulders, not about to let a surly teenager intimidate him. "I'm here to meet with some soccer club owners about coaching. Is your mother at home?" He forced himself to keep smiling while gritting his teeth.

"Who's at the door, Zach? Oh... wow." Another boy appeared, a young, male carbon copy of his mother. His dark eyes flashed. Then he barreled past his brother and pulled Metin into a hug. "Oh my gosh! I missed you!"

The surprising contact brought the sting of tears to Metin's travel-weary eyes. He held onto the boy, letting himself have a moment of happy memory before the darkness beckoned.

"I missed you too, Tanner," he said into his hair as Zach disappeared inside. "So, I'll ask you. Is your mom home?"

Tanner led him into the house, past a giant, slobbering brown bear he claimed was "just a Labrador named Bruce," and they sat at a small kitchen table. When Melanie appeared, the urge to sweep her into his arms was so intense it confused him, but he knew that would never do, not if the deep suspicion in her gaze was any indication of her frame of mind now that he'd actually shown up.

He had come to thank her in person. Nothing more. But the way he wanted to hold her, to kiss her, right in front of her sons, made his skin flame hot. Alicia's face wafted across his memory, as usual. He squeezed his eyes shut to dispel it, then opened them and forced himself to re-affix the smile.

"Hey, well, um, I just now read your email so... ah...." She ran her hand through her wet hair, her discomfort palpable.

Zach stood at her shoulder, his jaw clenched as tightly as his fists. "Mom, why is he here?"

Metin stayed quiet, despite his urge to smack the kid upside his disrespectful head.

"He's here to interview for a coaching job." She spoke to her son, but stared at Metin. "That's all. He wanted to stop by and see you boys. Since he hasn't in... so long." She dropped into a chair. "Relax, Zach. And if you can't, then go outside or something."

Tanner bounced up and down in his seat. "Metin, why don't you play for Real anymore? I saw when you punched that ref! That was totally awesome!"

"No, Tanner, it wasn't awesome, it was bullshit. Especially since he was drunk off his ass—again." Zach spoke for him.

Metin raised an eyebrow. The tension between mother and son was so thick he could almost see it shimmering and poisoning the air.

"Zach, that's enough. Metin went through a very tough time, you know that. Now back off. Just... go somewhere else, and let me talk to him a minute."

"Zach is right," Metin said, putting a hand on Mel's that lay, jittery on the table between them. "I acted badly and as a result, no decent club will touch me. I did it to myself. But I'm doing a little better now. Not great. But better."

He smiled at the boy and then faced Melanie. But he stopped short at the expression on her face and spent a moment second-guessing his motivation for coming here. Her dark gaze was somber, unhappy, and not a little bit pissed off. "Um, so, anyway." He took his hand off hers and sat up straight, collecting his thoughts. "I'm thinking about moving here to coach the expansion team in Detroit."

"Wow! That would be so awesome!" Tanner's voice broke in the way of boys becoming young men. "I heard Rafe Inez is in on that, too. Didn't you play with him once? He's helping Zach get scholarships. And they got Nicco Garza to play for them. You guys really hate each other, don'tcha? I heard about some other players coming from Europe. Do you know them?" He quivered with excitement, his grin comically wide.

"Shut up, you idiot," Zach growled from across the room. "You don't know what you're talking about. Metin won't stay and coach a team of nobodies like those Black Jack dumb-ass whatevers. Pro soccer in this country is a joke."

Mel looked so exhausted and beaten down at that moment, Metin had to bite the inside of his cheek not to pull her up and into his arms, something he absolutely would not do. He'd come there to make peace, to establish himself as a friend, or at the very least, rebuild a small part of his family again. It had taken him several weeks to get past her visit, and his visceral reaction to her. He wondered more than once what might have happened if he'd done something different that moment in the hallway.

No. He'd done the right thing. He needed Melanie in his corner, as his friend if he were ever going to recover himself. Jumping her bones the way his lizard brain kept urging him to do would have ruined that possibility forever. Full stop.

He kept his voice mild. "Zach, what I will do remains to be seen. There's no need to talk like that to your brother."

"You know what? Fuck you. You're not my... you're not anything to me. Not anymore. You were a colossal dick the last time we saw you." Breathing heavily, he advanced on Metin, who rose with hands at his sides. "You pushed my mother," he said, his face beet red. "At her own sister's funeral. And now I think you should leave. Crawl back into the bottle where you hid for two years and leave us the hell alone. No one wants you here. Trust me, I've heard my mom say it enough times."

Metin rose to his feet, his desire to put this kid in his place never stronger. But he stuck his hands in his pockets and mentally counted to ten, his temper pounding in his ears. He realized matching the kid word for word, when he'd said nothing that wasn't true, would only make a crappy situation worse. Besides, he was only doing what he thought he should do—protect his mother.

Mel spoke first. "Zach, I don't need you to do this. Metin and I have made our peace."

Metin mentally startled, hearing the words he'd been thinking fall from her lips. Zach wouldn't take his eyes off Metin's. "Stay away from us. I mean it." The young man looked like he could haul off and start punching any minute.

"You're overacting, but I don't blame you," Metin said, his ears still buzzing with fury.

"Do not psychoanalyze me, you selfish prick."

Mel slid between them just as Metin was about to grab the boy and shove him into the wall. This he knew and remembered well. The Matthews women and their infernal hands-off, anything goes approach to parenting. But Zach was correct about one thing—Metin had no say whatsoever in the machinations of this particular family, and anything he did would be misinterpreted, anyway.

"Zachary, go upstairs. Now." Melanie stood her ground, staring up into her son's eyes until they flickered away from her gaze. She put a hand on his arm. "Honey. It's okay. I swear it. I... we...."

At the look of desperation on her face, Metin took a step back from the two of them. He blinked, his head awash with emotions he couldn't pin down.

Friends, former family, this is what you are, nothing more.

"Oh. My. God," Zach spit out. "Mom. Please tell me you aren't fucking this guy." His blue eyes flashed as he sidestepped Mel and made for Metin.

"Zach, shut up!" Tanner shot out of his chair and launched himself at his brother, fists flying. Because he caught Zach off guard, he was able to knock the bigger boy on his ass and proceeded to pound on him. They rolled around on the kitchen floor, cursing and beating on each other while Metin and Mel watched, speechless.

"I'm glad to see the drama quotient around you hasn't changed," Metin said. He waited until things progressed a little too far then he waded in to pluck Tanner off of Zach. The younger boy's arms flailed and tears streamed. "Tanner, it's okay. Zach doesn't know what he's talking about. And he needs to leave the room before he makes me mad."

Mel put a hand on his arm, but he pulled away. "Let me handle this. I'm intimately familiar with being the youngest brother trying to beat the living shit out of an older one who deserves it."

He walked into the family room and plunked Tanner down on the couch, crouching in front of him then handing him a tissue. "Take a breath, Tanner. It's okay."

Zach scrambled to his feet and ran out the door, slamming it so hard it rattled the framed photos on the wall. Tires scratched out into the quiet suburban street. Mel dropped back into her seat at the table. Metin patted Tanner's leg while the boy calmed. Bruce, the bear-dog, lumbered in and slobbered all over his arm. He smiled. The Matthews family drama never ceased to amaze him. The animal shoved him off balance, onto his butt, making Tanner giggle through his tears.

The rightness of the moment, despite its inauspicious beginning, hit him hard in the chest. Metin smiled, and when he caught Melanie's eye as she walked over to help him up, he had a small flicker of hope that perhaps everything would all be okay, somehow.

"Can you eat dinner with us?"

Metin startled at Tanner's question. He was already headed for the door, figuring he'd done what he could, and needed to get on with his decision about staying in Michigan.

"Tanner," Mel said. "I didn't have any plans for..."

"I can cook," Metin said, turning around, eager to stay for reasons he didn't feel like naming.

"Since when," Mel said, her arms crossed, her smile wary.

"Since I have this," he said, pulling his phone from his pocket. "There's this cool thing called Grubhub. Maybe you've heard of it?"

"Shwarma!" Tanner yelped.

"No, no, I can make something," Mel said. "I've got burgers we can grill."

"So you're staying?" The young man's face was so open and eager, it hurt Metin's soul for a moment. This was good. It was fine. He missed Tanner and even the surly Zach who'd be sure to show up in time to eat if he knew teenagers and their appetites. He looked at Melanie, willing to let her make the call. The odd, crackling thing between them that had freaked him out when she'd been in his condo had calmed. It felt more akin to a warm evening with a hint of thunder hovering around the horizon. He was happy to be here with her and Tanner, but if she told him to go, he would go.

She sighed, looked up at the ceiling and muttered something under her breath, then met his gaze again. "Stay," she said. "But make yourself useful." She turned away and headed for the kitchen.

"Let's kick around," Tanner said, snatching a soccer ball from somewhere and tossing it to him. He caught it without taking his eyes off the gentle sway of Melanie's pink sweat-pants-covered hips.

He shook his head.

No.

Off limits.

Wrong. Wrong. Wrong on so many levels they can't be counted.

"Let's see what your mom needs us to do first," he said, tucking the ball under one arm and guiding Tanner into the kitchen ahead of him as a sort of human shield against his urge to do things that shamed him. She was slamming stuff around on the counter, the set of her shoulders and general demeanor not one that boded well for a nice, relaxing, family dinner.

"Mom," Tanner said, approaching her. "You okay?"

"Yes, I'm fine."

Tanner shot Metin a look. For his part, Metin's pulse was racing in a way he usually associated with pre-match jitters. But one thing he was one hundred percent certain of: when a woman said she was "fine" the way Melanie just did, it was either a lie or a trap. He reached for Tanner's arm and tugged him away, handing him the ball before pointing him toward the back door before looking back at her. Melanie had both hands on the black granite counter, and her head was bowed as if she were saying a prayer.

"We're going to go outside for a bit. Do a kick around."

"Fine," she said again, not looking at him, not even raising her head.

"Melanie," he said, moving closer. He didn't want this to be awkward. Just because Tanner wanted him to stay didn't mean she did. She turned to glare at him. He raised both hands and put some distance between them. "Right. Outside. That's where we'll be. Let me know if you need any help."

She snorted and started unwrapping a package of ground beef. Metin took that as a sign to get the hell out of her sight, at least for the time being. But his heart was light as he ran down the back steps to the decently sized stretch of green backyard.

"Incoming!"

Metin grinned and reached out to block the ball so it wouldn't slam into the back door then tossed it back to Tanner. "All right, you ready?" He stripped out of the jacket he'd worn over the open collar, soft cotton dress shirt, draped it over a patio chair, and started rolling up his sleeves. The boy's smile was a mile wide as he made a piss poor attempt at juggling.

"Ready if you are," he said.

Metin started jogging across the lawn, holding out a hand to indicate he was ready for a pass, and it felt like coming home.

Chapter Seven

Mel squished the ground beef between her fingers, determined to get this done, feed him and get him on his damn way—straight out of her life. She had no room for him or his... his... hotness and his inappropriateness and his...

She glanced up and caught sight of him whipping off his no doubt designer jacket, placing it gently on one of her chairs, then unbuttoning and rolling up his dress shirt sleeves.

"Show off," she said under her breath, as a shiver ran down her spine at the sight of his forearms as they appeared, one by one. He tugged his shirttail out of the black jeans that hugged his ass so perfectly they were probably tailor made. Metin Sevim was a whole lot out of shape. Even she knew that. She'd seen him enough times when he was in peak condition.

The irony of the whole situation—okay, one of them—was that she knew what it would take for him to get back to the place he'd been physically. She had basically raised her sister and Alicia had been athletic practically since birth. The horror of their mother's slow descent into death had changed a lot of things about their family, but the main thing was that she had to be in charge of her sister. So she knew exactly what it took, from carefully curated nutrition to alternating days of puke-inducing speed, agility, and weight training. Not to mention endless skills work with the team. The hours she had spent hauling Alicia around, sitting at practice sessions doing her homework or dreaming about the day when someone would take care of her had been long and boring. But she was thinking about it as she gawked at the sheer beauty of Metin's ball handling skills in her little yard with her non-soccer-inclined youngest son. He needed to eat a lot of protein and hit the gym, in a big way, if he was ever going to restore himself.

She blinked, realizing that he and Tanner were both waving at her. Frowning, she got back to her task and pounded out four over-sized hamburgers for the grill, then chopped some sweet potatoes to roast, and rinsed off lettuce and spinach for a salad. The entire time aware that the man she had hated with her entire being for so long for giving her little sister a perfect, fairy-tale life was in her yard right now, whooping and hollering with her son, and about to eat a meal on her patio.

And she was looking forward to it.

"God damn it," she muttered. Leaving the lettuce and spinach to dry on some towels, she wrenched open the refrigerator and grabbed a cold bottle of Sauvignon blanc. She spent about three seconds convincing herself not to do it then opened the damn thing and poured herself a healthy splash. It was a bad idea, but she couldn't help but walk to the window overlooking the backyard, wineglass in hand, to enjoy the view.

"Oh god help you, Melanie Matthews Miller, you are a horrible, terrible, very bad person," she said between sips. But god help her, but she did enjoy the view. Metin's too-long hair was whipping around as he dribbled the ball around the yard, basically playing keep away from Tanner while the kid laughed. The man's full lips moved as he spoke, mesmerizing her without hearing the words. A sheen of sweat covered his light brown skin. Mel licked her lips, imagining what it would taste like. His eyes shown. He was obviously enjoying himself. And so she decided it was okay to watch and enjoy, and appreciate. Because that's all it was—her appreciation of a truly gorgeous man. It would never be anything more. It couldn't be. She wouldn't allow herself to contemplate it.

He was her dead sister's husband.

Period.

End of discussion.

"Oh... crap." She groaned and gripped the edge of the countertop at the sight of him stripping out of his dress shirt. But when he shook his hair, sending sweaty droplets flying, then looked right at her, she knew he knew she'd been gawking at him. "Fucker." She turned away from the window, drained her wine glass and stomped to the fridge for more. She poured, sipped, and smiled to herself. It was a relief on some level to have him around and know that she didn't have to waste her energy hating his guts. But even as she held that thought in her mind, she realized her own reasoning for hating him had everything to do with something she'd lost and would never get back.

The tears came and the hitching sobs shocked her with their ferocity. Images flashed in her memory—Alicia as a little girl in her soccer kit, as a grown woman and successful pro player, her beautiful wedding in Istanbul, and her adorable little boy. "Oh... god," Mel said, as the wine glass slipped from her fingers and shattered into a zillion pieces at her feet. "I'm sorry, Alicia. I'm sorry. I'm sorry."

She heard herself screaming. Felt herself slipping to the floor. Sensed the shards of glass under her bare feet, and the slipperiness of her own blood. But she couldn't stop. She'd done the worst possible thing—had the worst possible thoughts about Alicia's husband.

"Mom!"

Mel heard Zach's yelp of concern from far away. The glass hurt her feet, but she ignored it as she curled into herself, wrapped her arms around her bent legs and sobbed.

"Mom," his voice was closer now. His arm around her shoulders. "What happened?" She shook her head, unable to catch her breath.

"I'm... it's..."

"Here," a deeper voice said from somewhere on her other side. "Take this." She heard a crinkling noise.

She shook her head again. "Try it, mom."

Still gasping, her brain spinning and her guts churning, she took the paper bag from Metin's outstretched hand and started breathing into it. It's not like she didn't believe it would work. It was more about her embarrassment at her outburst and the thing that had caused it—her own breathless horniness at the sight of Metin's bare chest.

Keeping her eyes shut, she breathed slowly in and out, until she'd restored the balance of oxygen in her body. "Ugh," she said, staring down at the total mess she'd made. "I've got to clean this up." After taking a single step, however, which lead to yet another slice into her instep, she let loose a string of curses at herself. 'I don't know what's wrong with me," she finally said, looking up into the three sets of eyes that were staring at her. She swiped at her eyes, furious at herself. "My god damned feet are cut all to hell."

Without a word, Metin took a step towards her and scooped her into his arms.

"Hey!" She said it at the same time Zach did, but for different reasons.

"Just be quiet, will you? I'm only saving you from getting your feet shredded." He marched into the adjacent family room and dropped her onto the couch. "Where's your first aid stuff?"

"Here, mom." Tanner handed her a towel that she put under her bleeding soles.

"I'll get it," Zach said, before zipping up the steps and back down while she sat in uncomfortable silence, mortified by the whole scene.

"Thanks, honey." She took it, rummaged around for some hydrogen peroxide, then took a look at the damage. "Crap. I need tweezers," she said even as she tried to yank a few of the bigger shards from her flesh. "Ow, shit!"

"Let me," Metin said, shifting the ottoman so it was in front of her and holding out a hand. She stared at it, then into his eyes. "Come on, already. Give it up." He made a "give it here" motion with his hand. She sat back and put her left foot on his thigh, determined not to notice how nice it felt to have his hands on her.

"No, stop," she said.

"What?" Metin looked up from his mission of de-glassifying her foot, his confusion genuine.

"Nothing," she said, crossing her arms and trying not to look like a pouty toddler. "Ow!"

"Yeah, that was a deep one. Okay." He patted her leg and held out his other hand. "Next?" She stuck her other foot on his lap and suffered his close attention until it was freed of all the shards. "Now you can use that." He pointed to the ancient bottle of hydrogen peroxide.

She soaked a couple of large gauze pads from the kit and pressed them to the bottom of her feet, one by one, wincing and hissing until the pain stopped. "I don't think I have this many band aids." She shook the box and three or four of them dropped onto the couch next to her.

"No, you sit, slather your feet with this stuff." Metin found some antibiotic ointment and handed it to her. "We'll finish the dinner, won't we?" She sighed at the sight of Zach's stony expression, and the sheer delight on Tanner's face.

"Are you serious?" Zach asked her, jerking his chin towards Metin.

"I invited him to dinner," she said, feeling defensive and then pissed off about that. It was her damn house, after all.

"You're insane," her oldest son said. "And you... you're... you're just..." His face turned red with the effort to come up with something scathing enough for his former uncle, the soccer super star he'd once idolized.

"You're in charge of the grill," Metin said. "I'm in charge of the salad. Let's go. I'm starving."

Zach clenched and unclenched his fists, looked at Mel, then at Metin's retreating back. She shrugged. "So, go be in charge of the grill." She started slathering on the ointment. He heaved a giant, typical sigh. "Look, I know it's a little odd having him here, but—"

"Odd? That's a funny word for it."

"Can you just not, for one night?"

He glared at her. She met it and raised it by a thousand, willing back the frustrated tears.

"Fine," he said, stomping into the kitchen.

She smiled, and finished treating her battered feet, leaned back and stretched her arms out. Tanner appeared, holding a recharged wine glass. "Metin says to give you this so you won't be so bitchy."

She frowned, but was unable to hold on to it in the face of her son's grin. "He's probably right."

She took the wine, sipped, and listened as Tanner and Metin cleaned up the mess, chattering away in her kitchen, while Zach slammed the door multiple times going in and out to deal with the grill.

The dinner itself wasn't completely awful, only a bit uncomfortable. Thankfully, Zach had "somewhere to be" in the way of teenaged boys, so he ate and ran, leaving her, Tanner, and Metin. When the door banged shut, they looked at each other and exhaled in unison. Tanner giggled. Metin drained his glass of water and got up for more while Mel turned the glass of wine around and around on the table.

"Can you stay for ice cream?" Tanner asked. Metin glanced at Mel. She shook her head. They'd spent enough weird quality time together. He needed to be on his way. She needed to get a shower, re-treat her wounded feet, and sleep for a solid eight hours. She'd already alerted her manager she wouldn't be in for the breakfast crowd, which would make them short-handed.

Metin ruffled Tanner's hair. He carefully brushed it back into its messy state. "Sorry. I have an early start tomorrow."

"Oh, right, with the Detroit team."

"Yes." Metin glanced over at her. She was still sitting at the table, nursing her last glass of wine. The intensity of his dark gaze sent an involuntary shiver across her scalp. She curled her fingers into fists, pressing her nails into her palms to distract her. She would not do this. She couldn't go any further into anything like what her fevered imagination kept throwing at her.

Alicia's laughter ghosted through her brain. She shut her eyes, exhaustion boring into her soul. She was so fucking tired of being sad, of carrying around all the baggage of being a sister, a daughter, a mother, a stressful business owner while never letting go of the raw fury that would light up her never endings whenever she thought about Metin. Except, she hadn't had that feeling since she'd so-called rescued him in Istanbul. And she sure hadn't felt it today. No. Today's heat didn't come from anger. It was gut deep, distressing yet undeniable lust.

"Metin has to go, Tanner," she said, her voice sharp. She slid her feet into the soft slippers Zach had brought her, then limped to the sink where she dumped the nearly full wine glass, rinsed it and stuck it into the dishwasher. When she turned, they were both staring at her, surprise on their faces. "What? It's late. He has to be in Detroit tomorrow, right, Metin?" She tried to relay her deep need for him to get out of her house with a meaningful look in his general direction.

"Right. Yes. That. I just need to get my jacket." He headed for the back door. She followed him, hesitating a moment before closing the door behind her and catching up to him. It was a shabby excuse for a patio, with plenty of moss and other green stuff growing up between the uneven pavers. She couldn't help but mentally compare it to the lush gardens, pools and fountains of his parents' home. But she got distracted when he tugged his sleeves down and slipped his jacket on. That irritating tickle of lust slithered down her spine once again, warming her in places she'd gotten good at ignoring for the past few years.

He stood, staring at her long enough to make her realize she'd been staring at him for the last few seconds in silence. Like some kind of loser. She crossed her arms. He crossed his, letting his expression match hers—somewhere between bored, neutral, and pissed.

"Thanks. For your help, I mean," she said, her voice scratchy. She cleared her throat and moved a few steps back so he could walk past her. He didn't move.

"You're welcome. It was nice to be here, to spend time with you and, well with Tanner, anyway."

He ran fingers through his dark hair, making her throat tighten in response. The cycle of emotion between anger, frustration, and desire was making her dizzy. She sighed and looked up at the darkening sky.

"Yeah, Zach is what he is." She shrugged.

Metin's eyes narrowed for a second, then he seemed to get over whatever it was and he echoed her sigh. "I assume you know where he's gone. Who he's with."

"Yes, thanks for asking. All good there." She'd forgotten this side of him. Alicia had complained about his strict parenting with Ayden, worried about what would happen when the boy became a teenager. Not that he ever got that chance. "Anyway. Um, see ya around. I guess."

Metin's shoulders slumped. He stuck his hands into his pockets and kept looking at her in a way that made her both hot and bothered. "Listen, I don't know what's happening here but..."

He held up a hand. "Nothing is happening, Melanie. I apologize for making it seem that way." He brushed past her, leaving her sweaty and shaking and somehow mad that he hadn't. What? Made a move on her? Grabbed her and kissed her senseless?

"Good. Okay. Bye," she said under her breath, following him back into the house. He gave Tanner a tight hug, then smiled at her. He seemed calm, completely unaffected by whatever the hell it was that swirled between them. Zach had picked up on it. Tanner, thankfully, was oblivious because it was god awful and it needed to stop right now.

She pulled Tanner to her. "Good luck tomorrow," she said.

"Thanks. I'll keep you posted." He headed for the door.

"Wait," she said, walking over to him, needing to get it out into the open. "Tanner, honey, will you get the dog off the couch and take him for a walk?"

"Sure, mom. Let's go Brucie boy." The giant, overweight lab groaned but flopped onto the floor and followed Tanner through the kitchen to the back hall, where his leash was hanging on a hook.

She waited until she saw the boy and dog walk past the front window and head down the sidewalk before she looked at Metin again. As she was opening her mouth to speak, to tell him to go, for good, and never return to her house, he blinked, then without a word, reached for her hand and pulled her to him. She hesitated, resisted, but it was too much. What willpower she possessed had melted away. Her breathing was loud in her ears. The sensation of his touch burned her hand, then her elbow, when he cupped it with his other palm.

"Melanie."

She blinked and realized she was staring down at their feet. His in a pair of trendy dress shoes with white soles. Hers in a ratty pair of slippers to accommodate her stupid injuries. Not very sexy, she thought, à propos of nothing and everything at that moment. He let go of her hand and touched under her chin, forcing her to look up, into his eyes. The anguish she saw in their brown depths made her suck in a breath and try to put some distance between them. But his firm grip on her elbow wouldn't allow for that.

"I...we...c-c-c-can't." She barely recognized her own voice. Confusion broke through the desire that was coursing through her, blazing all her synapses.

When Metin brushed a strand of her hair off her face and tucked it behind her ear, she couldn't hide the full-body shudder at his touch. "I'm not sure I know what to do with a Melanie who isn't bitching or berating me," he said, his voice low, musical with its once irritation-producing accent. But his words galvanized something in her. She reached for it, gripped it, and dragged it out of her, forcing herself to pull away from him.

"Yeah, well, I don't know what to do with a Metin who's trying to seduce me, instead of my sister."

His face contorted and his shoulders slumped. Mel wished she could yank the words back into her mouth at the sight of him. But at the same time, the relief at having dodged a potential kiss or worse with the man made her knees weak.

"Right. There she is," he said, crossing his arms. Mel took another step away from him in self-defense.

"Yep. Here I am. And there you go." She moved past him and opened the door. "Take care now, bye."

He hesitated. "I'm sorry. I shouldn't have come here."

"No, I'm glad you did. It was ... nice to see you and Tanner will live off that backyard soccer session for months."

"And Zach?"

"Oh, Zach hates everyone right now. Don't think you're special."

He smiled. She forced herself not to stare at his jawline, his shoulders, his hands. Dear god but she was horny. And this wasn't helping. Not one bit. That was surely her only issue. There was no way she had feelings for him.

Nope.

No way.

No how.

To her utter shock and horror, he pulled her in for a hug. His proximity almost made her faint. Since her nose was jammed against his chest, she sucked in a breath, filling her memory banks with the slightly sweaty, soapy essence of him. He pulled away first. She looked up and into his eyes. "Metin, I'm..."

The kiss shocked her. But after the first millisecond, she rose to the occasion, grasping his shoulders, wrapping her arms around his neck, molding herself against his slim, firm body. She parted her lips, inviting him in. His tongue teased her lower lip, then accepted her invitation. She sighed at the same time he moaned, turning them, pressing her back against the wall and slamming the front door shut.

He kissed her until she saw stars. Her hands crawled over his body, moving up his shirt to stroke the firm flesh of his torso. He reached down to cup her ass, gripping tight, grinding against her. But when she reached for his belt, he stopped her, breaking the kiss without a word. He glared at her for a split second, wiped his lips as if he'd tasted something gross, then yanked open the door and ran for his car. Leaving her standing at the open doorway, breathing heavy, her entire body ready for more.

He didn't even look back at her or wave. Just jumped into the rental car and screeched out onto the quiet road.

"Hi mom," Tanner said.

"Holy shit, you scared me," she said, meaning it.

"Sorry. Did you guys fight or something? He looked mad."

"No, we didn't. Go inside. I'm going to sit out here for a minute."

Her son shot her an odd look. She glanced away, mortified that he might have seen that stupid lip-lock, sad sack make-out session.

"Okay. Come on, Bruce," he said, tugging the slobbering, panting dog inside with him. Mel watched them go, and managed to wait for the door to close before she broke down and cried.

Chapter Eight

Metin watched the team scrimmage, noting without a hint of irony that he had never in his life seen such a rag-tag bunch of players. There were hints of greatness — Nicco Garza, one of them, although also the dictionary definition of "loose cannon." And that Parker kid, the one fresh from college, showed serious promise as a leader. As for the rest, well, they were exactly what Zach had called them—nobodies, mixed in with a boat load of has-beens and almost-beens.

In short, a shit ton of potential grounded in zero reality.

The sick part was he found himself more than a little excited by the possibility of pushing that zero towards a higher number. The concept of being a coach or manager or whatever they were going to call it was more intriguing by the minute, which shocked him until he realized that the memory of that damn kiss was still making him woozy.

He leaned in to Rafe at one point after observing a breakaway. "You know, I never understood why people would get mad and call me a showboat until now," he said as Garza nearly took out the goalie's testicles with a fierce slide.

The goalie, a bald, dark-skinned guy who looked as though he could eat Garza for breakfast, leapt up and throttled the old Spaniard, bringing both sides of the scrimmage into the scrum. Rafe put his whistle to his lips, but stayed quiet for a few seconds, letting them duke it out.

Finally, Parker, ten years younger than the average age of the rest of the team, waded in and separated the two, cursing at them both and shoving them down onto the pitch.

"I like that kid," Metin observed. "You should make him the coach." He kept his voice noncommittal, but if he were being honest with himself, the sights, smells, and sounds of the pitch were revving him up, making him want to jump into the fray himself. He wasn't sure if that was a good or a bad thing, but at least it kept him from obsessing over the way Melanie's dark hair had draped over one eye, or how comfortable he'd felt in her house that afternoon. And of how much he wanted to kiss her again.

"I know this is hardly a dream come true for you," Rafe said as they watched the team trot off the field for water. Nicco stayed down, glaring at the goalkeeper who got up and gave him a hard push before stomping away to find ice for his oncoming black eye. "But I think we... that is to say... you can make something of this bunch. Honestly. You aren't a jaded manager or anything but a former player who was always captain of his team. Your coaches always called you a leader on the pitch."

Metin kept his gaze trained on the man sitting on the field by himself. "I hated that fucking guy," he said mildly, unwilling to engage beyond that. "It was mutual. And you honestly think he'll let me coach him?"

Rafe glanced down at his clipboard, blew a whistle, and trotted out to the field to get the men back in line for some drills now that they had simmered down. Nicco stayed put, elbows propped on his knees, glaring straight at Metin.

"Well, what are you waitin' for, Garza, an engraved invite? Get your ass over here with the team," Rafe hollered. The man rose slowly, shot a salute Metin's way, then made his way over to the gathered group.

Metin sighed and took in his surroundings. They were practicing in an American football stadium at a small college near Detroit, but so much money had been procured by this Jack Gordon fellow that a brand new, state-of-the-art facility was being constructed downtown, a few blocks from a river front park.

It would house the team and a women's club, The Lady Jacks. He cringed at the name, mainly because he could hear Alicia's snort of derision over it. The facility, though? That was top shelf. There were giant, positively luxurious locker rooms, a state-of-the-art weight room, an office complex for the many departments it would take to run this new venture, several bars, a brew pub, and anything else one would want or need in such a place.

Metin squeezed his eyes shut. He hadn't felt the absence of Alicia so keenly in a long time. It hurt everywhere. He wanted nothing more than to talk to her, to get her no-nonsense advice about this bizarre opportunity.

And to kiss her—yes, that too—very much.

Behind that desire to see, hold, and kiss his dead wife, recent memories of Melanie rushed in, making every inch of his skin hot with a combination of embarrassment and lust. He'd avoided her completely for the last couple of days, letting himself be wined and dined by the money guys, accepting their condolences with nods and smiles and silence. Thinking the entire time that there was no fucking way he would do this. The list of reasons not to was several hundred kilometers long. He slumped down onto a bench, pinching the bridge of his nose, confused by the weird feelings he was having about Melanie—a woman he'd once claimed would just as soon slice open his ball sack as look at him.

Because right then, he wanted to call her, text her, to get her advice about what to do with what was going to be a huge paycheck to do a job that these guys seemed to think he could do. But could he? Was it anything approximating a good idea to stay here, near Melanie and her family, given the thing that seemed to be happening between them? What would her father think? Never mind her surly teenaged son.

He sat and watched the men go through their paces for the second half of training, impressed with some, aghast at others. Narrowing his eyes, he forced himself to get real and acknowledge a core fact — he was flat-out, gut-deep, afraid to return to Turkey. It was the scene of his failing, and he didn't think he'd ever be able to walk into that penthouse condo again without dropping straight into a hole filled with bad habits just waiting to cushion his fall to the bottom.

At least in Detroit, he had a goal, a focus. And there was Mel. He smiled, recalling how comfortable and happy he'd been with her and the boys, at least for a few hours.

Perhaps he was sublimating his grief by focusing on an entirely inappropriate woman. But Melanie Matthews, once a woman he went out of his way to avoid, would not exit his thoughts. And not just for physical reasons. The time they had spent talking, easing into something comfortable with Tanner over dinner, soothed him late into the night as he did his usual insomniac battle with memories.

Once the show and tell with the team was done, they headed back to the construction site that was quickly transforming into the Black Jacks stadium. Metin found himself sitting across from Rafe, and the immaculately dressed money guy. They were both trying to seem nonchalant, but he could sense their eagerness rising into the air, enveloping him, luring him in. Images of the lonely, empty, soccer-less life waiting for him back home filled his mind, tempting him. Melanie's face, laugh, the set of her shoulders and the way her lips tasted when he'd given in and pulled her close intervened. He blinked fast, trying to clear her out, to think like a professional, not like a sappy, needy, useless man.

"We've sent an offer package to your agent," Jack said, leaning back in the camp chair, one ankle propped on the other knee, linking his fingers behind his well-coiffed head. Dude looked as comfortable in a bespoke suit as if he were wearing weekend comfortable shorts and a t-shirt. Metin couldn't help but be impressed.

As if on cue, his phone buzzed with a text. He glanced at it. "Yes. She says she's got it."

"But we didn't want to let you leave without one last pitch," Rafe said.

Metin looked at him. He'd played in Copa, the South American league, for a few years. Got hurt and moved to the states to go to University, he'd learned at dinner the night before. Jack had brought him in to help him recruit players and locate a manager, and they'd ended up brothers-in-law.

Rafe's wife and Jack's sister Maureen was a beautiful, female version of Jack with inky black hair, blue eyes, and a big personality. She'd been seated next to Metin at dinner and he'd enjoyed the hell out of her company.

He sighed. "Okay. Pitch away," he said, trying to square the excitement about this possible venture rising in his chest with his anxiety over kissing Melanie. If there was anything in the world less appropriate than the way he'd behaved that night, he'd be damned if he knew what it was. But he also had to acknowledge that a small part of him was relieved that he hadn't spent the last forty-eight hours obsessing over all the things he'd lost. Instead, maybe, just maybe, he could find something new.

He shook his head. No, Nothing would ever replace the perfect life he'd had and shame on him for even thinking such a thing.

"You all right?"

He blinked, realizing that he had both hands clenched tight and his fists were digging into his thighs. His jaw hurt and he sensed a headache lurking. "Yes. Sorry." He forced himself to unclench everything, and take a deep breath without appearing to take a deep breath.

Jack leaned forward, elbows on his knees, fingers intertwined. His expression was serious. "I can't even begin to imagine what you've been through. No one can. I realize it must seem ludicrous for us to push this so hard, considering your situation." He glanced back at Rafe, who nodded, then focused on Metin once more. "But I can't help thinking that maybe switching your focus to something new, to something that has a different sort of potential might be a good idea. We've made a generous offer, and it includes a lot of perks like a housing allowance. We're new, of course, and don't have the kind of dough an established team could offer, but I think it's fair."

Metin's phone pinged with another message from his agent. It contained the basics of the offer. He read through it twice, then rose and held out his hand. "It's more than fair, Jack. And I promise that I will seriously consider it."

"The rookies need your experience and the veteran players need your guidance," Rafe said, shaking his hand. "It's a good fit."

Metin nodded. His head was pounding now. He wanted Alicia. He needed Alicia to tell him how to handle this. But Alicia was gone and was never coming back. He rubbed his temple to try to dispel what he realized he wanted—to talk to Melanie and bounce this whole thing around with her.

He'd spent his entire adult life being told what to do. Starting with his parents, all his coaches and trainers, then his agent and yet more coaches and trainers. Was he the sort of man who could do that? Provide leadership for a young, ragtag team with plenty of promise but a hell of a lot of unknowns?

"I'll get back to you within two weeks," he said.

"Sounds good," Jack said, opening the door of the makeshift, soon-to-be office onto the hallway. The sound of clanging and banging and other random construction noises filled his ears. Metin walked a few feet, stopped, and turned to look back at the two men who seemed to want him here so badly they were throwing a lot more money at him than he'd anticipated.

"It's not about the money, you know," he said. He shoved his hands into his pockets.

"I didn't think it was," Jack said, crossing his arms.

"This isn't some kind of mercy hire, Metin. We want you to know that," Rafe said.

"Feels like a life line," Metin said. "I just need to decide if I should grab it, I guess."

Jack and Rafe stayed silent. What else could they say to that? He nodded, pulled his phone from his pocket, and turned away from them again, heading towards the exit and the parking lot. He sat in the car, breathing heavy, heart racing as he tapped out a message to Melanie:

"I'd like to take you to dinner before I leave."

He waited a few seconds, then added, "I need a friend right now. Nothing more."

He pressed his forehead to the steering wheel, warding off the compulsion to drive to the first bar he could find and get blind, stupid drunk. His phone buzzed. He looked at it. Melanie had responded.

"Okay. Come out to A2, though. I won't be done with work for a while and I'll need a shower first."

• • • •

MEL CURSED AND RAILED and generally did her bitchy boss thing the day before Metin was to go home. She hated that the fact his presence mere miles away affected her at all. Much less the raw, physical way it did, right this minute. She took out her edginess on the staff, unable to stop herself.

She and Zach hadn't exchanged more than three words in the last few days, which hurt her feelings and pissed her off in equal measure. His accusation had hit her hard in the gut. Even after their nice and surprisingly relaxed dinner, especially after that kiss.

She sighed and slumped against the wall near her tiny office. The kiss had been a lot of things, not the least of them, transformative. The man's lips were soft but determined and the way he'd held her in his arms.

No. Stop it.

She pushed herself forward, forcing it out of her mind, thrumming with enough lusty energy to power a small city. When her brain helpfully reminded her that she'd agreed to dinner with him tonight, as a farewell or whatever, she groaned and pressed the heels of her hands into her eyes.

An hour before they closed, she sat, looking out onto the busy State Street hustle and bustle, Metin's dark eyes looming in her brain. She ran her hands over a smooth mahogany tabletop. Her palms fairly burned with the memory of the way his silky hair slipped between her fingers. She crossed her legs, embarrassed, mortified, and sick at her own seeming inability to purge him from her sensory memory bank.

Grabbing her phone, she hit his number, typing out a text before she changed her mind. This had to be, as they say, nipped in the bud. She would not allow it to progress a single step further, for her own sake. The words "second string" kept popping into her head. And "replacement player," and all sorts of nonsense phrases relative to the game that was still such a part of her life, thanks to her sister, her son, and so many others. She would not be that for Metin Sevim. No fucking way.

Sorry. Can't do dinner tonight. Have a safe trip home and stay in touch.

She hit send and started to power the phone off before focusing on ripping the lazy bartender a new asshole. But Tanner and Zach would flip out if they couldn't reach her, so she left it on, determined to ignore any message from the annoyingly handsome Turk who would not vacate her dreams. He tested her resolve within minutes.

Metin: *I really need to talk to you. About this job. I don't know what I should do.*

She shot back, "You're a grown man, Metin. Do whatever you want."

Metin: *I don't want to go home. To Turkey, I mean. That much I know.*

She rolled her eyes and firmly suppressed a slight flutter of excitement.

Nope. She had no business feeling that. None at all.

Melanie: *Then don't. But don't move here expecting anything from me.*

Metin: *I am sorry for what I did.*

Melanie: *Well, it's not like I stopped you.* A flash of memory slammed into her—his lips, his hands, his firm body pressed to hers.

Metin: *Mel, I swear I won't touch you, but I need to talk to somebody about this, and you're the one person who'll give me a straight answer.*

Melanie: *I don't know a damn thing about soccer clubs or leagues or any of that. I barely understand the rules, and only because I watched Alicia play, and now have to watch Zach.*

Metin: *Humor me.*

She frowned, trying to climb back onto her high horse and rebuff him.

Melanie *Fine. But someplace completely public.*

Metin: *Ok Where?*

Melanie: *Not my house, not here at the restaurant. No place that could have any dark corners. You know what I mean. Don't be obtuse. Your email was one of the most erudite ones I've ever read.*

Metin: *Yes, I read and write English better than I speak it sometimes.*

A few seconds later he followed that up with: *Please.*

She put her hand over her lips. What in the hell was happening to her?

Melanie: *Let's just talk on the phone. I don't think we should be in the same room for a while, you know?*

Metin: *Never mind. I don't want to put you out.*

She frowned, stuck earbuds in her ears, and hit the call button, unwilling to play that game.

"What?" he answered, his voice rough.

"Don't pout, Metin. I'm only doing this to protect us both. We don't need to be messing around anymore. Especially not here."

He blew out a breath. "I don't want to put you out," he repeated.

"You're not. Now tell me the pros and cons of this thing, and let's see if we can figure out what makes the most sense."

She put her head down on the table wanting nothing more than to have his arms around her which meant she was doing the right thing, keeping as much distance between them as she possibly could. He didn't care about her. And if he did move here, she would have to maintain that distance. Best set those boundaries now. But she shivered hearing his voice which she took as not a good sign for her resolve.

He laid out the terms of the contracts, the money—a number that made her curse under her breath then berate him for continuing his poor-little-rich-boy lament—the team's particulars and his opinion of their chances in a professional league, and finally, the housing allowance.

"You could get a nice place downtown for that," she said, staring down at her clenched fists.

"So I'm told," he said.

The silence after that comment lasted eons. Mel bit the inside of her cheek to keep from filling it with stupid chatter. They were well beyond that. But it was getting tough to ignore the signals her body was sending. Signals that reminded her how much she wished she were a different person, one who didn't have a dead sister named Alicia the soccer star who'd married the soccer star now breathing in her ear through the phone right now.

Because if she were that someone else, she wouldn't hesitate to invite herself over to Metin's hotel room right this minute and work this just-under-the-surface itch to tackle him to the bed out of her system and get on with her damn life. She was, in a word, horny. Shifting her chair in an attempt to dispel it and ignore the heat building in her core and between her legs, Mel blurted, "Well. So what are you going to do?"

He sighed. She shivered in response.

The man is a thousand times off limits to you, Melanie. He's your flipping brother-in-law. Stop fantasizing and get your shit together right fucking now.

"I need to go for a run," he said.

"Well, okay, then. Do that. Sounds like a good plan."

She winced at how lame and unhelpful she sounded. "I mean, it will clear your head, right?"

"Right." His voice sounded small and happy. Very unlike the man himself who was large, athletic, and one of the most persistently positive people she'd ever known. Her heart began to thump harder.

"Metin, I... we... we can't..."

"I understand, Melanie. I won't bother you again. If I decide to move back here, I'll steer clear of you and your family. Goodbye."

"Wait," she said, jumping to her feet and grabbing her phone as if that would keep him on the line. But it didn't. He'd ended the call without another word.

"No less than you deserve," she muttered to herself.

Chapter Nine

Metin sat in front of the open balcony door in his hotel suite, the sounds of a reviving city floating up to him on the breeze. Detroit had become one of the places people used to scare kids in Europe. As in, don't be naughty or I'll send you to live in Detroit with the arsonists and the killers.

Things had most definitely changed for the better. Now that he was seriously considering relocating here for good, he had to admit that his sense of identification with the place—of a city rolling over and letting the light shine into its many interesting nooks and crannies as it regained strength and prominence—had a lot to do with his frame of mind. He took a breath and propped his feet up on the adjacent chair, wincing as his hamstrings cried out in agony. Getting back into shape had proven harder than he'd thought, and fighting the urge to pop open a beer or sit at a bar and have five or six martinis in a row took a lot out of him.

He stretched his arms up, relishing the way his muscles ached. He felt alive again, something he'd never believed he'd feel. The pain in his soul would never cease. He recognized that. But living with it versus letting it control him seemed like an actual possibility.

He'd even starting chatting in his head with Alicia, usually late at night. She remained as bright and real to him as she had been the first second he'd laid eyes on her, at a party sponsored by her father's company. But his son, Ayden, the amazing thing they had created, he refused to remember. Because that one thing, the thought of his sweet laughter, his little-boy wonder at the world, his crushed potential, would send him spiraling straight into a black hole, never to return.

The conversation with Melanie, though brief, had helped, although he was still vacillating between staying put and running back home with his tail between his legs. No, the conversation had helped him in a different way. To feel connected to something he'd lost. He'd begun to recognize that fact meant more to him than anything. And he was a little pissed she cancelled their dinner, even though a bigger, more mature part of him understood why.

His scalp tingled at the memory of her lips and body, firm and slim, pressed to his. He shook his head. Melanie was off limits. They would be friends, and that was enough, because it had to be. Anything else was out of the question for more reasons than he could name. He steadfastly ignored any other thoughts of her, as tempting as they were.

Metin picked up the paper copy of the contract his agent had sent him and stared at the high six-figure salary. An astonishing sum considering the start-up nature of this whole thing. They wanted him. That much was clear. An antsy feeling crept up his spine, forcing him to his feet. He did some sit-ups, then push-ups, then stared at the television for a while, then wandered out onto the small balcony.

A sudden fresh rush of images hit him between the eyes, unwelcome and horrifying. He could see her, hear her—his Alicia. He felt his son's arms around his neck, his warm, small weight against his hip.

"Metin," she said. "Metin." Her firm voice demanded his attention.

He gasped, crouched down, fingers clenched together, wishing he were the praying type.

"Alicia," he ground out through a clenched jaw. "I'm sorry. So sorry." His gut churned with guilt at his own behavior, all of it, from the ignominy of the ruined career to the kiss he'd shared with her sister.

The breeze lifted the ends of his hair, caressed his cheek and bare chest. He rose, gripping the cool metal railing, holding on for dear life as the face of his one true love flashed bright, her golden curls, blue eyes, full lips as clear as day. He sucked in a breath, willing it gone, like a cramp. But it resisted his attempts until he flinched at the sound of a knock at the door.

"Metin," his Alicia whispered. "I love you. Please go and be happy." And she disappeared, as if someone hit a delete button on a computer screen, sucking her and his son into the void.

He heard the knocking again, firmer now. Muscles trembling as if he'd run twenty miles, his heart and head pounding, he walked to the door, opened it, and tugged Melanie into the room, slamming the door shut behind. He held her close in a desperate attempt to dispel the memory of Alicia's voice, his body hardening, his lips forming words he couldn't hear.

• • • •

MEL BLINKED AT THE sight of Metin in the doorway, wearing only shorts, his deep olive skin glowing with sweat, his eyes wild as if he'd seen a ghost. A warm breeze blew into the room, ruffling his dark hair, which he'd been wearing much longer than he had while married to Alicia.

She set her shoulders, prepared to give him some sort of excuse for driving all the way into the city, other than the fact that she had to get her hands on him. But before she could speak, he pulled her into the room, had her pressed against the wall, and his rich, delicious lips were on hers.

He kept muttering something like, "I'm sorry. I'm so sorry. Please make it stop."

Her logical brain rebelled for a split second. Until she accepted that she'd never in her life wanted anything more than to be here, doing this with the man holding her right now. And she wasn't about to stop.

She wrapped her arms around his neck and let it happen. He picked her up, back-walking until he sat on the bed. As soon as she was straddling his lap, she rose to her knees, hovering over him, staring into his dark eyes.

"I need this," she insisted, justifying it in her head. "Just this. Nothing more." Her heart pounded in her ears. He nodded, and lifted her shirt up, popped open her bra and flung them both to the floor. His lips touched one nipple, then the other, sending shivers down her spine. "You understand what this is, right?"

"Evet," he whispered as he nuzzled, sucked, and nipped. "Sí, mi amore."

"Do you have protection?" she managed, weak all over from his close attention to her eager nipples. He threaded his fingers in her hair, then licked and kissed his way up her neck to her lips. "Seriously, Metin, you've fucked every Eurotrash skank possible. How do I know...."

He stopped, tilted her face down to his. "Alicia is the only woman I have ever not worn a condom with. Ever. I swear it."

She recalled the sight of all the used ones she'd seen lying around the pigsty of a flat where she'd found him. But the sound of her sister's name coming from his mouth threw her. She backed away, rubbing her freezing arms, horrified by her embarrassing nudity, her raw, pulsing need. He sat, gazing at her, his body at full attention. She tried not to stare at the erection tenting his shorts.

"I get it, Melanie. It's just sex. Come back here. Let's have some," he insisted, but his eyes betrayed his flippant words. The actual emotion in them terrified her and drew her in at the same time. Mainly because it mirrored her own—which meant she had to reject it. She refused to feel anything for this man other than lust.

But her brain kept yammering at her, reminding that this could turn into something more. That she owed it to Alicia to put her damn bra back on and get the hell out of this man's hotel room.

She stepped away, shaking her head. "Metin. I know you. You get attached and I can't. I mean, we can't. It's too... oh, hell." She took the three steps between them and shoved him down, her hand and lips on his shaft, loving the pure maleness of him, the way his hips moved at her touch, the way he threaded his fingers in her hair and held on for dear life.

A blow job wasn't sex. It meant nothing. She'd suck him off and be on her way. Because the getting attached thing was clearly not one-sided. Mel shuddered at that realization. And that she simply had to do this thing, dispel the need that had roared its way into her life, then make a clean exit, never to return.

He groaned, yanking her up to face him. "I must be inside you, Melanie. I must."

He caressed her face, bestowing the most gentle, erotic kisses she'd ever experienced. No rushing, no urgency— only his lips and tongue, soft, probing and seeming to question her, which she answered by throwing her arms around him again. He turned them, eased her down, keeping his mouth on hers, his hands on her breasts, waist, and hips. Her panties and skirt had melted off her at some point. He stopped, poised between her legs, his eyes so dark and full of meaning she wanted to cry. She ran her fingers through his hair.

"I won't do this if you don't want it. God knows I love a good blow job." His smile was wicked.

"If you don't get this inside me in the next few seconds, I will flip us over and take care of it myself," she whispered, running her hand up and down his cock.

"I'll consider that a yes," he said, moving slowly, easing into her, never taking his eyes from hers. "Is it? Melanie?" His voice was low, his gaze hypnotizing. She cradled his face between her hands and lifted her hips to meet him. He sank deep, his lips on hers again and they rocked together in a rhythm as if they'd been together for years. She felt tears forming, but she forced them back. This was a one-off, one time only, a one-night stand.

And it felt so damn good.

"Yes. Yes. Yes. Yes!" she cried out as her body pulsed around him at the same moment he groaned and buried his face in her neck. His hips moved a few more times, then he looked at her, his expression sheepish.

"I'm not usually so selfish," he said, pulling out of her and flopping onto the bed. "Ugh, I'm doing everything wrong."

Mel chuckled and ran her fingertips down her breasts to her stomach. "Oh, I came, no worries there."

"I know you did, but I prefer that you have many climaxes before I...well, anyway." He draped an arm over his eyes. "That wasn't very good, and I apologize."

"Metin, I haven't had sex in so long you're going to have to take my word for it when I tell you it was great. Exactly what I needed. I hope you feel the same way." She heard the weird formality of her words, but her brain was scrambling, seeking an exit lest she tuck herself into him and let him cuddle her.

Metin pulled her close, and she went, of course, weak willed cow that she was. Sleep was stealing over her. Maybe a tiny little nap. "Shh. It's fine. Rest," he whispered into her ear.

"Nope." She sighed, rolling away from him onto her back once more. "I gotta get home."

He ran a finger down her face and neck, to her breast. "I'm going to take the job." Leaning in, he kissed the line of flesh he'd just touched, unable to stop.

She jerked away from him. "I hope it's not because I came here." Leaving the bed, she clutched the sheet to her body, her face flushed red, her thick, dark hair a mess. "Because we, um, did this. Even though we shouldn't have. And we won't ever again. Shit." Her voice broke.

· · · ·

METIN TRIED TO KEEP his own voice even and calm. It wasn't easy. Melanie brought out a lot in him—lust, satisfaction, and no small amount of frustration. "Well, I was on the fence. You could be accused of shoving me over."

"Well, get back up on the damn fence, Metin. I'm sorry. I shouldn't have come here." She scrambled around for her clothes.

"No, I'm kidding. Relax. I had already decided. But you did seal the deal nicely for me."

"Oh god, oh Jesus, oh hell." She sat on the edge of the bed, her shoulders slumped, a tear rolling down her face.

He got up, slipped into his shorts, and crouched in front of her, desperate not to ruin this moment because it suddenly felt very crucial to him.

He took her hands in his, noting that she was trembling. "Melanie. It's okay. I'm not going to ask you to marry me or anything."

She shot him a strange look. "I get it," he said. "I can do a just sex thing with you. It's fine. It's more than fine. It's good for us both, I think. But I do ask one thing of you."

His skin burned. His heart pounded with fear that she would walk out, that he'd made the fatal error of having sex with her and ruining what could have been a solid friendship, and the connection to his past he so desperately wanted. She'd just shown up to talk, most likely. He suppressed the urge to groan at what he'd done. And the stronger urge to do it again and again, to huddle there with her forever, skin to skin, emerging only to eat and shower for the next week or two.

She raised an eyebrow at him. Encouraged, he leaned forward, running his fingertips up her thighs, which made her groan and flop back onto the bed. Which gave him an instant rebound hard on. He bit back the urge to crawl up her body and show her what he meant when he said, "many climaxes." He sucked in a breath instead.

"You have to consider me a friend. That is, someone you call on when you need something, or someone to talk to. Okay?" He tried to keep his voice even, calm, not reveal how much more he wanted from her.

She propped herself up on her elbows and stared at him, her dark hair covering one eye in a way that made his dick even harder. "Friends, eh? Pretty clichéd, this benefits thing, don't you think? Can we be that? Fuck buddies?"

"I'm sorry, I don't understand." Her scent made him crazy-horny all over again. "But if it means we don't fight, and we get to fuck like this on a semi-regular basis, count me in." He dropped to his knees and yanked the sheet aside.

"God damn it," she exhaled. "Okay, deal."

He grinned against her flesh, sucked her clit into his mouth as he slid his fingers into the sweet glove of her body, drawing an operatic orgasm out of her. When she rose to her knees and shoved him onto his back, Metin felt something in him release its tight, agonizing hold on him. He blew out a breath, stared up into Melanie's dark eyes, and kissed her as she straddled his hips and lowered herself onto his aching cock, one delectable inch at a time.

• • • •

NAUSEA SLAMMED INTO him at the sight of the Delta terminal of the Detroit Metro Airport. The last two times he'd been here, he'd been blind with agony, deaf from devastation, and running away from everything, hoping he could drink it gone. When his phone dinged with a text, he jumped.

Melanie: *Don't get freaked out at the airport, Metin. I know you are. So stop it. Things are different now. You're fine. You're going home to pack. Take a breath, get some coffee and a magazine with pictures of half-naked girls. You'll be fine.*

He grinned and tapped out his reply.

Metin: *Damn you're bossy. How do you know I don't have an older woman fetish and am doing this to prove to you what a young man can do?*

Her quick response had him grinning from ear to ear as the iron band that had fastened itself around his chest the moment he'd walked away from Alicia's hospital bed loosened a tiny bit more.

Melanie: *Huh, and how do you know I'm not a voracious cougar looking to use you up and discard you? Now go on. See you in two weeks.*

His smile dissolved into a frown.

Metin: *What are you telling your family about us?* He wasn't sure what he meant and regretted the words the second he hit send.

There was a longer than usual pause. He cursed himself for asking.

Melanie: *There is nothing to tell them. We're friends. What we do on our time is none of their business.*

Fair, he typed. But his ears buzzed with a familiar something he identified later, as the plane rose into the Detroit sky to take him home to pack. A sort of possessiveness and the alarming sensation of wanting her family to know the whole story so that they didn't have to sneak around. But he dismissed it as ridiculous romanticism.

They would never be anything more to each other than a great lay and, hopefully, remain good friends. He drifted off, the familiar lull of flight sending him to sleep, and dreamed of Melanie—her face, her laugh, her smart mouth and her incredible lips and body as they all worked in tandem to draw him slowly towards the light of something new—waking when the plane bumped to a stop in Amsterdam.

Chapter Ten

By the time Metin had his hands around the team, his new life in Michigan, and the way he felt about Melanie, everything seemed to slide into place. At the two-thirds mark of the season, he'd coaxed, cajoled, threatened, begged, and shoved his rag-tag team into first place in the expansion league, but more importantly, they had won every single "friendly"—soccer talk for "exhibition," match, at least at that level.

They'd even defeated a top Major League Soccer team, the Canadian national team and, ironically enough, the Istanbul team where he'd humiliated himself what felt like ages ago. Not a bad start at all. Their crack marketing and public relations departments were getting them all sorts of buzz, including a fair bit of annoying gossip, which meant they truly had arrived. Once people started giving a shit about whom the players were fucking, marrying, and breaking up with, everything changed. It was something Metin understood well, having been the topic of gossip for much of his adult life.

The whole thing had its share of headaches, of course. With a team consisting of "been there, done that," players mixed with youngsters fresh out of college, the opportunities for trouble abounded.

He had a stack of personnel issues a mile high most days, and the team's recent jaunt out to the West Coast, stopping to play games in Portland, Denver, San Francisco, and Las Vegas, hadn't helped. He had plenty of hotel staff complaints, a couple of quickie weddings and subsequent divorces, and one drunk and disorderly that he suspected was something he needed to address with the team psychologist—the usual bullshit considering the level of testosterone they were dealing with. Luckily, the powers that be had hired a crack legal staff, so Metin could mete out punishments on the field as he saw fit, and let legal handle the rest.

He swiveled his leather chair around from the window overlooking the large, colorful pitch. The damn game was one part actual football and ninety-nine parts show business, which bugged him. But as Jack Gordon liked to remind him, it paid his salary. So he did his job and did it well, it seemed, at least so far.

His desk was tidy, with player files stacked to one side, recruiting info on another. But devoid of anything personal, of course. Whose photos would he display? His dead wife and son? Maybe one with his dead wife's difficult sister, with whom he had maintained a steady stream of sex, sex, and more sex. Their official status, Friends with Favors, as they liked to call it, maintained through four solid months without letting up.

He smiled and leaned back in his chair, propping his trainer-clad feet on the desk top, giving in to the temptation of recent memory, until he realized that particular trip down memory lane was going to force him into the locker room and under a powerful stream of cold water. Glad of the decision he'd made over the last few days. It was one his parents and brothers would no doubt chalk up to another "attachment issue," but he didn't care. The traditionalist in him kept rising up, choking him with a strange possessive feeling about Melanie that he didn't have the energy to fight anymore. It was no longer in him to sustain the status quo. He wanted more and suspected she did, too.

He slid open the middle drawer and stared down at what he'd placed there earlier in the week, as if it could quell his nervousness. This was what he wanted, what he required, and he believed this step could fix him, shove them both past the final stages of loss.

An annoying, tiny voice piped up, reminding him that rushing into anything more permanent with Alicia's sister might not be such a hot idea. Especially considering how much fun they were having. Why mess with that? Cursing his inner traditionalist—the one who craved normalcy, a stable home life, like a starving man craved protein—he pondered his next move and how it would either be the best or the worst possible one ever in the history of men doing truly stupid things.

"Metin." He flinched, hearing his name from the hall outside his office. "Um, sorry."

Surprised, but not unhappy to see Zach standing at his doorway looking sheepish, he shut the desk drawer and beckoned the young man into his office. "Hey, Zach. What's up? What are you doing in Detroit on a school day?"

"It's a testing day for juniors so we don't have to go." The boy kept blinking, fiddling with his backpack strap.

"Well, okay, come on in, have a seat. I was about to watch some film to see if I can figure out what the hell is wrong with my goalkeeper lately."

The commonality of their mutual love for soccer seemed to put Zach at ease. He sat, and they watched for the better part of an hour, talking strategy and identifying that the tall, black, completely bald man in the goal for the Black Jacks must have injured his left knee and wasn't coming clean about it. They had lost their last match when the opposing team seemed to have figured that out before Metin did, continuously aiming soccer-ball-shaped bullets right to his weak side.

Metin also knew, thanks to the never-silent internal team gossip machine, that Tayo's girlfriend had broken up with him a week prior, which could also be part of his problem. He made a note in his calendar to have the man in for a chat, to see if he needed some time with the team's therapist. Metin was a huge fan of the emphasis the Black Jacks ownership put on ensuring the team's mental, as well as physical, health.

But the fact remained that the position of goalkeeping was not their strongest when it came to players off the bench. He pulled up his roster, frowning when he saw what he already knew. It was one of their weakest in terms of subs. He needed another keeper, a good one, to fill in while he convinced the man in question to get his knee, and emotional issues, addressed.

"Uh, listen, I was wondering," Zach interrupted his musings about stubborn players who played through injuries. "There's a girl, and I, um... I want to ask her out. I think she'll go, but." The boy glanced down, his thick brown lashes covering his eyes.

Floored that Zach would come to him for dating advice, treating him like a trusted older brother, if not a father figure, Metin swallowed hard, trying to summon anything that might sound useful. He tented his fingers together in front of his face and attempted to summon a wise expression. Zach stared at him, face red with embarrassment. The whole thing made a chuckle rise in Metin's throat, but he choked it back. Zach needed help and had come to him to get it. He needed to take this seriously. He rose, grabbing his phone and office key card.

"Let's go get something to eat. You should never try to figure out what to do about a member of the fairer sex on an empty stomach. That's my first piece of advice."

Zach jumped to his feet, his expression reflecting the sort of relief that Metin hoped he could live up to, because frankly, that was the only wisdom he had. A weird, guilty sensation coursed through him as they made their way toward one of the pub-style restaurants in the stadium. The place did a brisk downtown lunch business, and today was no exception. Shoving aside all the images of himself with the boy's mother and what they'd been sneaking around and doing nearly nonstop, he pointed to a table and ordered them both ice water with lemon.

Zach frowned at him at first, then shrugged. Metin laughed outright at that. "Please, Zach, I've seen your fake ID and your mother says you hardly ever come home on the weekends not smelling of alcohol. It's what young men do. However, as you have driven all the way down here, I can't allow it." He smiled up at the waitress.

Holding up his glass when they arrived, he clinked it to Zach's, and they sipped. He scrabbled around in his brain for useful words about women, choking and spluttering when Zach spoke first.

"I know you and my mom are together." The boy's face held no malice, only a calm acceptance as he put his glass down. "I came home early last Friday."

It was Metin's turn to blush and squirm. He'd received one of Mel's sexier texts that day and blown off a meeting with his bosses to race to her house to surprise her. She loved doing that to him. Fucking with his head via a few words typed out on her phone. Once she figured out he was a stone-cold sucker for dirty talk, she was relentless, many times insisting she talk him through an orgasm when he was on the road with the team.

His face burned with the memory of last Friday's encounter.

· · · ·

WHEN HE'D ARRIVED AT her house, she'd been folding clothes in the laundry room when he'd arrived, wearing a pair of shorts, a t-shirt and no bra.

"What are you doing here?"

He'd licked his lips and swept her into his arms, kissing her as if his life depended on it within seconds. Melanie was ravenous, insatiable, and had revived his own once-impressive libido in ways he'd never believed possible. He lifted her onto the folding table, shoved the towels and shit to the floor, and yanked her shorts off.

"I'm here because you want me to be here," he'd said, dropping to his knees and licking his way up the inside of one leg until he had his mouth exactly where she wanted it.

"Well, I didn't think you'd drive all the way out here. I'm, oh, okay. That works." She sighed and leaned back, propping her bare feet on his shoulders and tilting her hips to give him full access. He teased and sucked her clit, fucking her with his fingers until she came with a loud cry of satisfaction, her heels digging into his sweaty back.

He rose, wiping his lips, one hand on his aching cock. She looked at him, her color high, her hair falling out of its tie back. He reached for her, pulled her off the table and kissed her, giving her a taste of herself as she wrapped her arms around his neck and molded against him. He ended the kiss and cupped her cheek, staring at her, needing to say something but afraid to say it.

"Payback time," she said, tugging his shorts and underwear off and dropping to her knees. He leaned over to grip the edge of the washing machine, relishing the sensation of her expert mouth and tongue on his cock, bringing him to the ragged edge. But this wasn't what he wanted.

He reached down and pulled her up to her feet, shuddering when she gripped him with one hand, determined to finish him off that way. "No," he said, his voice rough.

"No what," she said.

"No more," he said, his heart pounding as he stared at her.

"No more what? What's wrong, Metin?" She let go of his dick, thank god since he was about to blow all over her hand. She leaned away from him, her eyes dark, her beautiful lips turning down.

"Nothing is wrong. But I want to..." He tried to get a grip on himself, to say what he'd come here to say. But before he could get a single word past his lips, she'd covered them with hers, her eager tongue prodding into his mouth, her hands all over him. His mind went completely blank and he let his body lead.

"Turn around," he said, breaking the kiss, turning her, bending her over the table and gripping her hips. "Ah, god but you are beautiful," he said, running his hands along her ass and reaching between her legs to feel her heat—the heat that he'd created. All his, this heat.

All his, this woman.

She looked over her shoulder and arched her back. He groaned and reached for her hair, yanking it out of the holder and burying his hands in it as he eased into her, slowly at first, clenching his teeth against the urge to come inside her within seconds.

"Fuck me, Metin," she demanded, her voice as hoarse as his.

He paused. She looked over her shoulder at him again. "What are you waiting for?"

He sucked in a ragged breath, dug his fingertips into the flesh at her hips and pounded into her, hard, again and again until they both came, her with a loud cry and a yelp, him with a shudder and a low groan. He stared down at her back, let go of her hips, and ran his fingers along her spine. Her skin was sweaty, so he leaned over to taste it, keeping their bodies connected as she shivered in the aftermath of her orgasm.

"Oh my god," she said, as he pulled out of her and leaned back against the washing machine, his legs weak, his mind blank and his heart pounding from the words he'd left unspoken yet again. "That was a lovely surprise visit. Thank you." She grabbed one of the freshly washed towels and wiped between her legs before reaching for her shorts.

"Yes," he said, moving slowly as if in a trance, his own post-orgasm stupor slipping over his consciousness. "I love you," he said, before he realized the words were going to appear. "I mean..." His ears were buzzing and his skin felt hot and tight all over.

She froze like the proverbial deer in the headlights, a frown materializing as he watched her withdraw into herself.

"No, Metin, you can't."

"Hey mom! You home?" Zach's voice broke the moment into a million pieces.

"Shit, shit, shit," Melanie muttered, shoving him aside to open the window to air out the sex that permeated the room.

. . . .

AND NOW, OF COURSE, he knew they'd been caught.

Speechless, because what does one say to the teenaged son of the woman you'd fucked six ways to Sunday and would happily fuck again, today, tonight, every day she wanted him to? Metin ran a hand across his lips.

"Yeah, so what I want you to know is, I'm okay with it." Zach grinned up at the pretty waitress who brought them their burgers. "I mean, in general. Maybe not so much the loud sex in the middle of the day. You know, in the laundry room."

He honestly wished for the floor to open up and swallow him, right then and there. But a small smile played around Zach's lips, so he figured he'd stay at the table a bit longer. He cleared his throat, but when he spoke, it came out squeaky and lame. "Right. Okay. Sorry about that."

"My mom has been through a lot. And believe it or not, I want her to be happy. I think she deserves it. And I assume you think that, too." His face grew serious, his eyes darkening. Metin's admiration for the kid ramped up, admiring how he protected his mother while encouraging her happiness at the same time.

He downed half his water, wishing it was a beer, or something stronger, even though since coming to the U.S., he'd stopped drinking cold turkey, forcing that self-discipline on purpose. A wave of worry about how he could fit into Melanie's reality washed over him, filling him with dread, even as he pictured the emerald and diamond ring he'd purchased a week ago.

"So, about my problem." Zach devoured his food as only a healthy teenaged boy can do. "Now that we've got you and my mom sorted out."

Metin laughed again, sounding hysterical to his own ears. "I am probably the worst guy in the world to ask for advice in this area. But I will tell you a few key things: One, don't be an asshole, no matter how many people tell you that girls are drawn to them. They may be, once or twice, but at the end of the day, you are better off with a girl who likes the real you."

"Fair," Zach said, dragging some fries through a puddle of ketchup.

"Two, do not, for any reason, believe anyone who tells you that 'no' means 'maybe.' If you're unclear if she even wants to kiss you, ask first. Ask more than once. And keep asking, every time you go to the next step. Do you follow me?"

Zach nodded. "So I have an idea for a first date."

Metin listened, ate, and got to know the young man who'd been a mere boy when he'd entered his life, married to his Aunt Alicia, and become his mother's mortal enemy. Once they got the kid's date plans straightened out, Metin stood, a strange, antsy feeling coming over him. They watched a bit more film, and he let Zach hang on the sidelines for the team's afternoon practice. By the time Zach was back in his car and headed to Ann Arbor, Metin decided the ring box would stay put where it was a bit longer. He wasn't even sure why, but knew that it had to be that way.

At five-thirty, his phone buzzed with a text. Somebody owes me something, Melanie said.

He frowned, his body going on high alert as usual at the sight of her first volley in the daily sext session. Suddenly not in the mood, he ignored it, changed into running clothes and forced an hour of laps around the field and then another hour of weights with the team. He collapsed into bed in his new house, one he'd purchased a few weeks before in one of the Detroit neighborhoods within cycling distance from the new stadium, exhausted in body and mind.

The chat with Zach had thrown him. But it was more than that. Swearing he would call her first thing in the morning and have a real discussion about where this crazy relationship was headed, he drifted off into a dreamless void of sleep.

He woke, sitting straight up in bed at one point, breathing heavy and wondering what had made him do that.

"Metin," Melanie whispered. "I missed you."

He lay back, watching as she entered his room and stripped out of her clothes. He welcomed her to his bed with open arms. They went slow for a change, him still half-thinking he was asleep and dreaming, but the sweet perfection of her body and the bright ecstasy of her all around him brought real tears to his eyes.

"I love you," he said again, stroking deep, shuddering while they came together. "Melanie."

The next morning, he woke to an empty, rumpled bed and the lingering smell of her. Melanie never stayed over, no matter what. He'd gotten tired of waking up alone because he did love her. Which said nothing about his love for Alicia. His wife, his very heart—Alicia was gone. He had to move forward and complete things with Melanie and her family.

He rose, resolved, a plan evolving in his head already. One he knew damn good and well was impulsive. But he had a point he wanted to make, in public, with her.

Chapter Eleven

The Black Jack Gentlemen's first season was a surprising success with Metin and Rafe at the helm, to the delight of locals and, eventually, the larger soccer world. The European press lambasted him for a while, for giving up and going as far down-market as he could get. Coaching, at an American club, in an expansion league, in Detroit of all places. But they had dominated, continuing to win both regular and exhibition matches. So the team planned to throw itself a fancy end-of-season party to celebrate, and to gain more media attention. Ever the goal, Mel was learning.

She followed the team's success, but from a distance, only attending one game and that because Zach and Tanner wanted to go. Thanks to Rafe's help, they were looking at three decent Division 1 scholarship offers, and Zach had become ever so slightly easier to live with. Mel suspected the appearance of a lovely girl named Gayle at her house with some regularity had something to do with it. But she didn't care as long as he used the food-club-sized box of condoms she'd given him.

So she knew her reaction to his request was not going to fit with all the happiness and success surrounding the man sitting across from her in a nondescript coffee shop on a Saturday morning after they'd had one of their usual wild nights of sex, some of it pretty damn kinky. He'd let her tie him to his bed, torture him a little with ice cubes and hot lube. She shivered at the memory. Plus, as far as she was concerned, they were friends, honest-to-god confidants. They talked every single day about everything under the sun. But with the season over and him at loose ends until recruiting started up again, she got a distinct sense he was unhappy with their arrangement.

She sipped her coffee. "I'm not going to a public event with you. I can't. People won't understand. It's too soon. Too weird." Her knees shook under the table. She wanted nothing more than to go, to be with him, for them to be seen together. But terror at the thought

96

of being considered the fill-in for the prettier, more glamorous, more soccer-worthy wife—her own sister, no less—held her back.

He leaned in, his dark eyes intent. "It's no big deal, Melanie. But I don't want to be the only one there without a date." He ran a hand down his face. "You are so damned stubborn."

She stayed silent for a long, awkward moment. What else was there to say? Finally, words formed. "We need to wait until Zach is off to school to be." She waved her hands around, at a loss for words. "Public, you know?" Her nerves jangled, anger mixed with frustration. Why did he have to throw off a perfectly good arrangement with his sudden change of attitude about it? And what, exactly, made her keep pulling him in, teasing him with sexy text messages almost every day, craving his body against hers every night?

She must be some kind of sicko. But every time she laid eyes on him, took in his strong profile, the deep brown skin, dark eyes, silky black hair, and those lips. Mel gripped her knees under the table to keep from yanking him into a side room right then and there.

"Whatever." He stood, tossing down some money. "As long as you understand that I'm not going without a date. So when you see something on Instagram or whatever, don't freak out."

She stared at him, openmouthed. A surge of painful jealous fury hit her between the eyes. She grabbed his arm. "Sit," she hissed. He stayed standing. "Please." He remained upright. "God, now who's stubborn?" She got to her feet, their bodies too close for them to be considered anything but lovers. But she didn't move. She didn't care at that moment who knew what about the two of them and their odd arrangement. "I'll go. How dressy?" She dropped back into the seat, defeated, ears clanging with too many emotions to sort through at the moment.

Sitting across from her again, he said, "I knew I could coax out your inner possessive female." He grinned and took a sip of his previously abandoned coffee.

She frowned, opened her mouth to tell him to perform an anatomically impossible act on himself, but he put his fingers to her lips, calming her. She bit one, hard, loving it when he cursed her and yelped.

"So." she batted her lashes. "What time? And how dressy?"

• • • •

THE BLACK JACKS WERE originally meant to be an expansion team located in Las Vegas. When that deal fell apart and the Detroit money came calling, they decided to keep the name. So it made sense for one of the Detroit casino resorts to sponsor the team—and to host their first end-of-season celebration.

The glitzy banquet hall sparkled with players, WAGS, and expensive china and crystal table settings—along with plenty of paparazzi. Mel took it all in stride, even though she was a nervous wreck, and felt every single gaze on her, judging her for being here at the coach's side instead of her soccer star sister. She stuck close to Metin, blinking at all the cameras and wondering if any photos of her would turn up where she didn't look like some gawping hayseed. She thought more than once about bolting out a side door and escaping, until she had to remind herself that she did, indeed, deserve to be here—that Metin wanted her here with him.

It didn't help that he'd been on edge the entire night, jumpy and snappish, even after telling her she looked good enough to eat in her black sheath and sky-high heels. She'd shaken hands with Jack and his wife, Sara, accepting their congratulations on the success of Ayden's Café. Received a huge hug from Rafe, met his strikingly attractive wife, Maureen. Trying to frame herself as, "just a friend, and yes, Alicia had been her sister" about a million times while people gave her sidelong glances and whispered behind their hands made her a twitching wreck by awards time and dessert. She soothed herself first with champagne, then with plenty of wine, and before she realized it, she was well on her way to shit faced.

Metin didn't touch any alcohol, drinking water instead like a man dying of thirst. She eyed him, sensing his nervous energy as if it were her own while the official awards were presented. Then the team gave each other paper plate honors. The kind teammates make up and give to each other by way of a roast to the loud laughter and applause of the black tie-attired group. To their coach, the team presented a plate covered in photos of running shoes cut out and stuck in it called the "Shut the fuck up or run" award. The press was all over it, blinding and deafening her with their flashing and clicking.

Finally, it appeared to be over. She sighed and turned to Metin. "I'm overserved and thinking you can take full advantage if you—mmph...."

He kissed her, hard, in front of the assembled group, which fell eerily silent. She pushed him away, furious, and terrified, and way too drunk to be dealing with any of it. He pulled her to her feet, then dropped down on one knee.

"Holy hell," somebody said to her left. "Reminds me of somebody I know."

She met Sara's gaze as the woman laughed and leaned into her husband's arms. They all watched expectantly. The room remained silent but for the pop of camera shutters. She shook her head, unable to compute what was happening other than she was about to make a fool out of herself, thanks to Metin.

"Melanie," Metin said, soft, low, sexy, and perfect. "Marry me. Please."

She bit her lip and turned, pushing her way out of the room. Stopping halfway down the hall, she gasped for breath, trying to keep the floor from tilting and tipping her over.

"Mel!" a voice called. She ran from it. She wouldn't do this. She didn't love him. She couldn't love him. He wasn't hers. He was Alicia's.

Guilt flooded her brain, then anger that he would put her in such an embarrassing position in front of all those people.

"Leave me alone," she choked out, trying to find the bathroom through her tears and a haze of way-too-much-wine. But he caught up with her in the wide, empty hall, held onto her, and kissed her, drowning out everything but him. He stopped, making her want to beg him for more, until she recalled why they were in the hall. She had run from him. Because he had done the most idiotic thing ever in front of the whole team and a phalanx of journalists, no less.

"I won't leave you alone. I'm done being a friend with favors. I mean, I will be a friend, with favors, who is married to you. Or nothing else."

She struggled out of his grip. They stared at each other about the same second she realized that five or six photographers had caught them in that clinch. How dare he do that to her? Her hand shot out, connected with his cheek. He barely moved and his dark, anguished face was the last thing she saw before racing out into the lobby while yelling for a taxi, her palm stinging and her own face burning with embarrassment.

"Wait, Melanie." A different voice hit her ear. She whirled around, ready to bite heads off or burst into tears. "Hold up a second." Rafe approached. His wife trailed behind him, concern in her eyes.

"I'm fine. I need to g-g-get home." She shivered, unable to stop. "I don't know what got into him, really. We're just... oh hell." She turned from them, unwilling to explain.

Maureen caught up with her and draped a soft wrap around her bare shoulders. Mel clenched her teeth, unable to accept any kindness at the moment. It was too horrible. Metin was Alicia's husband, her own sister's man, and now everyone knew she'd been screwing him. She hoped no one had figured out how hard she'd fallen for him in the process, and how that fact was so much worse than falling into bed with him.

"Oh god, I'm gonna puke." The lobby spun. Lights, voices, the booze all churned through her.

"Rafe, grab one of the cars." Maureen dragged her toward the ladies room and held her hair while she lost her dinner and cried like a stupid, weak loser. She stared into the toilet bowl, watching as it flushed away her dinner.

She groaned and flopped onto her butt in the fancy bathroom stall. "I'm so sorry."

"It's okay. So that was a surprise?" Maureen handed her a damp paper towel. Mel held it to her forehead, then wiped her lips.

"Yeah. Something like that."

"Okay, let's get you in the cab," Maureen said, all brisk and businesslike, holding out a hand to help Mel to her feet.

Mel attempted to focus on her. "Thanks," she muttered, wanting nothing more than to see him again, to make sure he was real, that he meant it. No one wanted her. She was the bitchy, older, bitter sister. Not the perfect, athletic, beautiful one. The fact of Alicia's death hit her again, as if it had happened mere hours ago. Even as she exited the bathroom and let Maureen steer her away from the gathered throng of reporters and cameras, she started shaking again.

Rafe helped her into the cab and knelt down before he shut the door. "Ease up on him, Mel," he said. "That was harder than you might think."

"Then why in the hell did he do it, I mean, like that, in front of everybody and the press, oh Jesus." Melanie averted her eyes and slapped a shaking hand over her mouth. Because she knew why. Metin had made it public to prove something to them both. She understood it, but she wouldn't allow herself to believe in something so perfect for herself. "You don't know anything about me, Rafe, but thanks for the advice. And helping me with this. Tell him...." She bit her lip. "Never mind." She shut the door and stared straight ahead. If she saw the couple standing there with pity in their eyes, she would scream until she had no voice left.

She woke to find both their pre- and post-proposal kiss photos splashed all over the gossipy, bullshit Euro-soccer news sites. It had made a small blip in the States, mainly so the whole back story, the ugly, deadly prequel could get dredged up, exposed to the light, then dragged over the coals. Photos of the golden couple of soccer at their fairytale wedding, the gorgeous baby, the three of them in Spain and Turkey were splayed all over social media and on the morning coffee and talk shows. These were of course followed by the ones from the accident—Alicia's demolished car, Metin lurching through some airport or another, blind drunk with grief, then one of her from the funeral, hanging on her father's arm, blood dripping from her nose.

Mel stood and slammed the laptop shut, forcing herself to move slowly, to be calm, to not pitch the damn thing out the nearest window. She picked up her phone, then put it back down when she realized that her first inclination was to reach out and check in with Metin. To ensure he was okay with the full frontal onslaught of it all, this horrible jaunt down memory lane. That urge alone forced a frustrated scream and multiple curses from her raw throat. Bruce, the dog Metin insisted was a bear in disguise, started licking her hand as he made soft whining noises.

She flopped into a chair, ignoring the beeping of her phone, the dinging of incoming emails, and let the dog do his best to soothe her

Finally, Zach came downstairs, rubbing his eyes and scratching his belly. "What's up?" he asked, poking around in the fridge for food.

"Zach, I need to tell you something." Mel sat frozen, terrified at what he would think, what he would say to her.

"If it's about you and Metin, I already know." He kept his back to her, as he pulled out a bowl of berries, some yogurt, and milk.

She opened and closed her mouth, unable to locate words that made any sense. She put a hand over her eyes and made a valiant attempt not to cry. "Well, it's nothing. And whatever it was, it's over. So, yeah." Needing movement to dispel the onrushing panic, she jumped up and stuck her feet into running shoes and headed for the door, not caring that it was all of thirty degrees outside.

"Mom," Zach said from behind her. "Relax. He told me. Asked me if I was okay with it if you guys got married. I assume you told him no, since he's not here." He licked his fingers, his handsome face wide, innocent, free of anger for a change. "That's too bad. I think he really loves you."

"You have no idea what love is. You're just...."

"I'm almost as old as you were when you had me." He stared her down, the mature wisdom in his eyes giving another unwelcome jolt of reality.

"Exactly. And yes, I said no. So, sorry, no soccer-star-for-a-former-uncle-slash-stepdad. Oh god, I've got to get out of here." She stumbled to the street, hitting her stride as the tears dried in the cold.

Chapter Twelve

"Okay, does anyone have any questions?" Metin rose and looked around the room, using his best Roy Kent-style, dark eyebrows, nobody ask me anything or else-intensive glare. He was a thousand percent not in the mood for questions or anything else. He wanted to put last weekend behind him and move on somehow, without Melanie in his life. Since it was painfully obvious now that all she wanted him for was sex, and had proven it to him while embarrassing him in front of the team, the media, pretty much the entire soccer world. He sucked a breath in between his teeth at the sight of not one, not two, but three different hands in the air. With an audible groan, he flopped back in his chair.

The whole Metin-is-a-grumpy-bastard thing had worked for him. It allowed Rafe, his second in command, to be the nice guy, which he was great at, but had also proved plenty effective if their finish to their rookie season was any indication. The owners were already offering him more money so he wouldn't bolt.

But at this moment, all he wanted to do was crawl home and brood, compose and delete yet more texts and emails to Melanie, then brood some more. He could sense himself sinking into a bad place. Not as bad as he'd been after his family was ripped from him thanks to a drunk driver, but damn close. Mainly because he'd been forced to relive the whole nightmare of a Christmas morning all over again, thanks to the ever-helpful press. It didn't help that the holiday season was looming like a huge predatory bird, ready to pounce and gouge out his eyes.

Partly your fault, you giant idiot, he reminded himself. You shouldn't have pulled that kind of public showy proposal. You had to know she'd never go for it.

He heaved a sigh and glared at one of the raised hands. "Yeah, what?"

"Coach Sevim, when are we adding the women's side?"

He squinted at the person asking, then grabbed the glasses he'd been wearing in lieu of the contacts he used to wear to play. "Why do you care, Mason," he said to the young man who was an up-and-coming midfielder. The kid had subbed in at some critical moments at the end of the season and proven himself worthy of a possible starting position soon, if he put on some muscle. Metin crossed his arms and deepened his glare. But to his credit, Hank Mason, one of the younger players, rose to his feet instead of shrinking away from his coach's famous, looming temper.

"I care because I think the women's game is just as important."

The room erupted in a combination of cheers and jeers. Metin let it carry on, noting that young Mason didn't back down. After a glance at Rafe, who gave him a miniscule nod—a communication tool they'd worked out over the course of their successful season—he leaned forward, hands on the table in front of him. "The Lady Jacks," he said with an inner wince at the awful name. "The women's side will be on board by the end of next season. Management is working on locating the right coaching staff at the moment. Next." He pointed to another hand, this one belonging to the team's official man whore—a term he hated but realized for what it was. "Jax."

"Coach." The guy looked around as if seeking support, ran his fingers through thick blond hair, then jammed his hands into his pockets. Metin raised an eyebrow.

"Do you have a question?"

"It's more like a comment."

The entire room groaned in unison.

"What," Jax said, looking around before fixing his gaze back on his coach.

"I'm waiting," Metin said. He crossed his arms, wondering what in the hell had gotten into the team today. They seemed anxious or antsy or something. The season was over and it had been way more successful than anyone imagined. Why not depart and start ripping a party hole in the city like he would have done, once upon a time. What was with all this BS hanging around for coach's question time.

"I think..."

"There's a first," some wise ass opined. Metin glared. The tittering stopped.

Jax's pale complexion betrayed him with a flush. He frowned, then grinned, reminding Metin why the damn kid was such catnip. After running his hand through his hair a few more times, he looked back at the table full of coaching staff. "I think we should do something nice, you know, for kids who'd never be able to come to a game here. Mabye let 'em, I don't know, run around the pitch a bit?"

"Oh, hell no."

Metin turned his head to see where that came from, unsurprised that it was Fred, their operations manager. He looked back at Jax, mentally flipping through the guy's personnel file. He'd come from poverty, Metin recalled, raised in some backwater Texas town, discovered by accident when he'd been spotted playing at school by an eagle-eyed club coach. He'd been moved to the rich suburbs and raised by a family in a different part of Texas once it was established that he'd been more or less living rough in a trailer, alone, since his druggie parents had dumped him there. He'd risen fast, played two years for a solid college program, then overseas first for Chelsea then Juventus and now, here he was. Their very own fair-haired golden boy—who'd managed to screw his way through a full contingent of groupie fans leaving heartbreak in his...Metin shook his head before he rhymed that one.

"I'll look into it. Next." He pointed to his onetime nemesis, Nicco Garza, even as he noted Rafe tapping away on his tablet, no doubt putting Jax's request in motion. He raised an eyebrow as Garza rose to his feet, wincing the way only a man of a certain age who was still playing this boy's game would. Nicco had surprised everyone, including Metin himself with his sudden change of heart about a third of the way into the season, and between him and Parker Rollings, they'd bullied this group into winning a lot of games. Metin knew it was due to their own burgeoning relationship, but that was something he refused to let the marketing department use as fodder.

Being the poster boys for "it's okay to be gay on the soccer team" was not something he would wish on anyone, much less these two men who'd become invaluable to the team's dynamic. He didn't care if they were a couple, but wishing pro soccer had a more mature view on it was not the same as the current reality no matter how much pink-washing went on when rainbows appeared on every damn thing in June. It would be ugly for them. And he was determined to protect them from the ugliness.

"Coach, I'm wondering if you need a hug." Nicco held out his arms. His smile was both wicked and somehow genuine at the same time.

Metin blinked. "What?" The coaching staff rose from the table. Metin gripped his knees, realizing this for some sort of ambush.

"You did something that, while a bit ill-considered, was brave. I admire your bravery in the face of rejection, and I know you're feeling low," Nicco went on. The team was also standing up and gathering in front of the table where he was now the only one sitting. "Come on, ya big ugly Turk. Give us a hug."

Metin rolled his eye but got to his feet and let himself get pulled into the group. It was odd how much these men meant to him. They'd beat every team that was supposed to wipe the pitch with them. And even though they'd lost a few matches that still gave him nightmares, the Black Jacks had seriously over-achieved. He felt his eyes sting, so he shut them, gave the shoulders nearest him a good squeeze, then broke the group hug. "Enough, already," he said, his voice gruff. "Go on, go party or something for fuck's sake."

"D on three," Parker shouted. Everyone reached in with one hand, Metin only a few seconds behind.

"One, two, three..."

"BJs!" the group shouted loud enough to cause a few people walking by in the hall to stop and glance into the room.

"That wasn't 'D,'" Metin said to Rafe as they waited for the team to make their way out of the room. It had taken him a few weeks to get used to calling the city "the D" but he'd encouraged its use for their team's hype cheer.

"Nope," Rafe said.

Metin turned to stare at his assistant, the man who'd been so determined to drag him back to the light of day as manager for this damn team and had proven to be the best possible first assistant. He was great at personnel management and other details that Metin didn't want to deal with. Their good coach, bad coach schtick worked pretty well. But sometimes he felt shut out of the sort of team dynamics he'd just experienced. "Are you going to explain it to me?"

Once the last man was out the door and the rest of the coaching staff was gathering up their tablets and papers, Rafe sighed and slumped against the edge of the table. "It's short for Black Jacks, but also blow jobs."

"Ah, right. Of course." Metin felt his skin heat up with a combination of memory and extreme regret. It was a combo he was getting used to when pondering his seemingly doomed relationship with Melanie. As it usually did, his brain coughed up memories of her, of them together, which didn't help. They'd shared some amazing times, including some with Tanner, pretending they were a family. He shook his head, castigating himself all over again. He was such a stupid fool, thinking he deserved a normal life, or anything that involved a normal family.

"Do me a favor," he said to Rafe as the two men were heading for the doors that lead out to the parking lot. He could hear the various expensive motors roaring away as the team departed.

"Only if you promise me that you'll consider my invitation."

Metin stopped and put his hand on the other man's shoulder. "I appreciate the offer, Rafe. Please let Maureen know how much it means to me. I honestly don't know what I'm going to do for ... it." He couldn't even bring himself to say the words "Christmas" or "holiday." It felt profane, like the worst possible insult, to consider having a good time. If he were being honest with himself, he had half planned to go home to Turkey where Christmas wasn't such a big deal—mainly another excuse to shop—where he could ignore the whole thing and his mother and sisters-in-law could baby him for a week or two.

"Understood. Let me know if you change your mind. What is the favor?"

"I want to start a club, a training one, for kids."

"You want to do what?" Rafe was blinking fast, as if his brain was trying to process the logistics already.

"Just hear me out. Jax's suggestion got me thinking. Why don't we have a club but not one that rich parents can buy their kids' way into? One that's only for kids who couldn't afford any of the super expensive clubs, but one we train up ourselves. A feeder team, in a way, but one that lets all kids play. I hate it that soccer is a sport that only rich kids can excel at here."

"I like it. Let me talk to Jack over the holidays."

"Sounds good." He held the door open. "I'll let you know about..." He waved his hand, indicating the words he couldn't bring himself to say.

"You got it, Coach," Rafe said, sparing him another hug, which was a good thing because Metin wasn't a hundred percent sure he could take it without begging the man to let him come home with him, to let him do something, anything not to have to go to his own echoing, empty house.

Metin stopped on autopilot on the way home and bought a fifth of bourbon and a case of some random, expensive, high-alcohol beer. He put it all on his kitchen table while he stared at it, his eyes burning, his pulse racing, inviting and tempting but, as yet, unopened. The hollowed-out sensation he'd lived with for so long but had rid himself of returned with a vengeance, dragging its claws along the inside of his chest and skull.

His phone rang. He ignored it, choosing instead to open the bourbon and skip the whole dirty-a-glass thing by tipping it right up to his lips. The first taste was harsh, the second less so. The deep maple and vanilla notes of his favorite Kentucky whisky eased a path to his brain, bringing even more clarity about how stupid he'd been to ambush Melanie with a public proposal.

He got up to pace, then wandered out into the cold night and started kicking the line of soccer balls into a small net he'd set up, whaling the shit out of every single one without realizing he was yelling until his next-door neighbor—a sweet old lady who brought him cookies once a week — stepped out onto her patio to inquire after his state of mind.

"Metin? Hon? You okay over there?"

"No, I'm not."

"Need me to come over?"

"No, Missus Grant, I apologize for being loud."

"Okay, then. But I'm here if you need me. I've got some homemade banana nut bread."

He flopped into a patio chair, not feeling the cold anymore. When his phone rang again, he stared at it, bleary and furious at himself for giving into the weak compulsion to drink. "What?" he barked into it, tipping the now empty bottle to his lips. "Shit." He wondered why there seemed to be two bottles in his hand and not one.

"Metin?" The sound of Melanie's and Alicia's father's voice stirred the dregs of deep, painful memory. "How are you, son?"

"Fine." He hiccupped. "Sir." He sank down in the seat, hand over his face, trying hard not to end the call. The man had probably lost what little respect he had left for him, anyway.

"I heard what happened at the banquet." Trevor Matthews's voice hadn't changed a bit from its James Earl Jones chesty intonation. "And I was wondering something."

"What's that, sir?" He shut one eye, trying like hell to make all the doubles of everything in his back yard become single again. Standing, he tripped over a soccer ball and nearly sent the phone sailing across the yard when he landed on his hip.

"What are you doing for Christmas this year?"

Metin sat up too fast. He leaned over his knees, now hyper aware of the freezing temperatures and his rising nausea. He got up. Then sat back down. Why in God's name did people keep asking him about this? Why did it have to be such a thing? Couldn't he just hide for a couple of weeks and let it all pass by him?

Trevor Matthews kept talking, spilling yet more incredible words into his ear. "We don't celebrate anymore, Melanie and the boys and I. Last year we got through the whole thing by heading down to a resort on St. Bart's. We've got the same thing planned this year. And I'm wondering if you'd like to join us."

He rubbed his temple, stomach churning at the thought of a second anniversary of the day his entire life came to an end. "I mean, thank you, but considering the current circa... circle... circums... I think it's probably not a good idea. I think you know why."

"I think you should join us, Metin. I'd like to see you again and I think that, especially considering the circumstances, it's important you spend that day with us."

He pressed his forehead against the cold brick exterior of his house. The house he lived in alone, rattling around in the rooms, using boxes for tables, a mattress and box springs for a bed. The bed he and Melanie had christened many times, along with several of the box-slash-tables. He tried to stifle a groan. "I'll consider it, sir. Thank you very much for asking me."

"You're a good man, Metin Sevim. I was proud to call you my son-in-law. And while I do question your sanity with regard to a relationship with Melanie, that's only because I find her so... well... terrifying. Not because of Alicia. I would support you two together, a hundred and ten percent. I want you to know that. And I believe that Alicia would want you both to be happy."

Metin had no words for that. His head pounded. He needed more alcohol. He needed to drink some water. He needed to get a grip.

He wanted Melanie so badly at that moment. He needed her calm, if slightly snarky ability to bounce him out of his gloom. But maybe she was right. Maybe it was the opposite of right, this wanting of things that should remain out of reach. Maybe he was a terrible person for thinking otherwise.

"I'll email you the details for the resort. I'll have a room reserved in your name. We're going down on the twenty-second as soon as the boys are out of school. We'll stay through the New Year. You are welcome for any part of that. But I'd rather you tell Melanie. If I do, she'll accuse me of manipulating her life, and I'm too old for that sort of guilt."

His words brought a smile to Metin's face. He leaned back against the house, wondering if he should ask the man who'd fathered two women he loved more than life itself. The one woman who had been snatched away from him in one snap of fate's fingers. But also the one who'd burrowed under his skin to the point that he was ready to drink himself into a stupor to forget her. "Sir," he said, his voice shaky, unsure how to ask what he needed to ask.

"I have no words of advice for you other than these: you have to follow your heart. I lost Alicia's and Melanie's mother years ago and haven't looked at, nor seriously contemplated, another woman since. I can't. It's not in me. But I'm not you. And following your heart is what I was told as I mourned Cathy. So I did, in my way."

"Thank you, sir. I'll um... I'll let you know about the holiday."

"Good man. Take care Metin. I'll see you soon." And he hung up, leaving Metin to ponder more booze, or sleep.

Making it as far as the couch, he passed out face down, his dreams a crazed jumble of women he loved.

• • • •

"OH MY GOD, DAD, SERIOUSLY, you did not invite him!"

Mel glared at her father, ready to pack and leave if Metin showed up. The boys were down on the beach, trying out body boards in the light surf. She sat, slathered in sunscreen and under a hat and sunglasses, trying like hell to relax, her foot tapping on the sand, a deathgrip on her tumbler of white wine, doing the exact opposite of relaxing.

"I did. But I don't think he's coming." Trevor was parked under an umbrella, with a book and a giant tumbler of gin and tonic.

It was December twenty-fourth, Christmas Eve, and for the second time in her life, she refused to acknowledge it as anything more than the twenty-fourth day of the last month of the year. Her heart already ached so much as the hours progressed it was making her breathless. She had no idea what Metin might be going through, but was determined not to care. She refused to ponder it for even a second, or she would lose what was left of her mind.

"Well, at least he has some sense." Disappointed and pissed for feeling that way, she watched the boys a while. "I'm sorry. I don't know how he and I... I mean... it's a little..... Oh, never mind," she managed to stutter out.

Her father put a firm hand on her arm. "Melanie, I want you to be happy. That's all I ever wanted for either of you. I still want that, and if it is this man who does that, who am I to question it?" He patted her hand, then returned to his book.

A small flame of anger flared in her chest. Why was she the only one in this equation who thought the whole screwed up situation was wrong?

"But Dad, why? I mean, isn't it weird or gross or, I don't know, somehow just wrong?" She drained the rest of her drink and reached for a refill from the bottle.

"It is love, Melanie, and the last time I checked, that wins out over weird or gross." He put his book down and glared at her. "You refused to accept anything about him when he was with Alicia. But he's a good man. Wanting to be with you doesn't suddenly make him a bad man. It makes him a man in love, pure and simple. Why can't you just go with that? You have got to be the most stubborn woman on the planet."

And with that, her father disappeared behind his book again, leaving her to gape at the cover where his face had been, questioning her motives for loving the man she'd claimed to despise for so long, and wishing for nothing more than to see him, to hold him, so they could help each other through the next few hours as the memories came flooding back, as inexorable as the tide.

They started Christmas day late, not rising until nine-thirty, then having brunch at the resort, then going on a long beach walk to clear the fog of mimosas that she'd over-served herself. The boys procured a soccer ball and slide-tackled each other in the sand for a few hours. Mel must have fallen asleep because one minute she was watching her sons play, and the next, one of them was shaking her awake, making noises about a locked door and Metin. She sat up too fast, the sun and booze sending a shaft of pain into her brain.

"What the hell are you talking about?" She rubbed her temples.

"Mom, Metin's here. But he's...."

She squinted at her son. "He's what, Zach?" She blinked, trying to get her bearings.

"He's banging around in his room and won't answer the door."

"I'll see what I can do." She patted his shoulder, trying to keep her voice light, detached, as if this were happening to some other family. But her heart was whamming in her chest and her temples pounded with a combination of stress and anxiety.

Without comment, she started up toward the resort. They had a detached three-bedroom condo, and her father had reserved a suite in the main building for Metin, if he showed. Shoving aside her own sadness at the day that loomed large, that absolute nauseating brutality of the moment when the police called her house that horrific day, she focused on the task in front of her. Her father met her halfway and gripped her arm, making her stop at his side.

"Go easy, Mel. You can be a little dismissive of other people's sorrow at times."

She scoffed and tugged out of his grip, squared her shoulders, and cleared her mind of anything. Anything but the fact of the matter: Metin had traveled here, and now he needed her help.

Chapter Thirteen

I t took her almost a half hour of knocking and cajoling and convincing, but Metin finally answered the door. She was about to give up, and was leaning with both hands on either side of it, staring down at the carpet when he ripped the thing open so fast she nearly fell inside. But she stepped away, determined that they wouldn't slide into their typical fuck first talk later habit.

"Wow, you look like shit," she said, meaning it. His hair was wild, his jaw rough. "And you reek. Did you sleep in those clothes for the last week, or what?" She brushed past him, not letting any part of them touch, and swept open the curtains and the large glass door to let in some fresh air. "How long have you been here?" She glanced around at the wreck of a room, the neat freak in her itching to tidy up the place.

He didn't speak, just stared at her. She repressed the urge to shiver under his dark gaze. "This was a bad idea," he said, dropping down to his heels, his back against the wall.

"Thank you Captain Obvious. But I'm not sure which bad idea you'd be talking about." She stayed across the room and kept her voice low, although the urge to run to him and hold him tight overwhelmed her.

"Coming here. Go away. Leave me alone."

She began collecting empty beer bottles. "No, I don't think so. Get in the shower. I'll clean some of this up."

"I said, go." He rose, his eyes snapping with fury or something like it.

"And I said no." Keeping it light, she continued to tidy. Her heart pounded when he drew near. A now-familiar hand gripped her arm, turned her around. She glared at him. "Get your goddamned act together, Metin. We're here to honor Alicia and Ayden, not drown ourselves in self-pity. I won't tolerate it. Get in the fucking shower." She ground out the last, hating herself for being such a bitch to the man, for not "going easy" as she'd been asked to do, twice.

After guiding him to the large bathroom, she helped him strip out of his clothes and shoved him under the shower spray. He stood for a minute, then met her eyes, propping his hands on the tiled walls. "Join me?" He raised an eyebrow.

"Not a chance. Get cleaned up. I'll order you some food."

She put the place more or less in order while trying not to break her arm patting herself on the back for not going with her gut and jumping in the shower with him. Then she called room service to order him a steak, some carbs, and a giant bottle of water. He stayed so long in the shower she worried for a second, but as she was about to check on him, the water stopped. He emerged a few minutes later, a towel wrapped around his hips, looking hungover, but cleaner, and as devastatingly hot as ever. Mel bit her lip and averted her eyes from the obvious tent under the cotton. He flopped into a chair opposite her, groaning.

"My hair hurts."

"Yeah, no wonder. Hang on."

She set up the food that arrived and put a hand on his bare shoulder. His skin seemed to sizzle under her palm, sending a shock wave of lust straight to her lizard brain. She took a breath, focusing on the need to be an adult, not a horny kid, at this particular moment. When he gripped her hand and tried to tug her around to his lap, she resisted.

"Nope. You need to sober up, eat, and sleep. Let's talk tomorrow. Okay?" She pulled out of his grasp.

"You still hate me," he mumbled. "I don't know what made me think you'd actually marry me. Jesus, what a fucking sap I am, huh?"

"No, not a sap." She crouched down next to him. "You're a wonderful man and I've really enjoyed these last few months. But we can't be together. You have to get that through your head."

But I want to be with you, her inner self screamed. After shoving Inner-Self-Melanie into a separate mental compartment, she locked the door with a firm click. She couldn't do it. He was doing it for the wrong reasons, for a start. And she deserved more than to be the replacement for her sister for him.

He scowled at her and she smiled, trying to defuse the moment. "Tomorrow is the second anniversary of the worst day of our collective lives. If you aren't sober for it, I will never speak to you again. Do you get me, Metin Sevim?"

"Fuck off. I'll do what I want."

She thumbed his chin, forcing him to meet her eyes, nearly biting off her own tongue to keep from kissing him, wrapping him up in her arms, and soothing him the only way she knew how.

"No you won't. Not if you're here with me, with my father and my sons. You made the trip down. Now get your ass sober, get some sleep, and we'll see you at breakfast." Unable to resist, she pressed her lips to his forehead, then his cheek.

He clung to her and all the familiar responses rose. But she disentangled herself. "Not tonight, Metin. And perhaps not ever. But we will get through this day and the next one. And we will be friends. Because that's what we both need, more than we need to keep screwing around. Now, do what I'm telling you. Or I'll get mad and you definitely don't want that." She left before she lost control and ruined it yet again with her own neediness.

· · · ·

METIN OPENED ONE EYE, then the other, relieved to find himself headache-free. He stretched and climbed out of bed, never more grateful for Melanie's bossiness.

As he stood at the large window, he spotted Zach and Tanner down on the beach, going one-on-one with a soccer ball. He smiled, right before reality sidled up and sucker punched him.

The day. Today.

The twenty-sixth of December had arrived, right on time, yet again.

He sat, trying not to hyperventilate. After a while he got up, found some jeans and a T-shirt, and wandered out to find the promised breakfast. The one space that looked like a restaurant was empty, so he made his way down to where he thought the boys were.

He spotted Melanie lounging under a large umbrella with a huge picnic spread out in front of her. Her father sat in a low chair, his face buried in a newspaper. Metin took a breath and walked into her line of sight. She smiled, and his heart lifted, ever so slightly from where it had been mired for two years in the muck of utter despair.

"C'mon on, then." She patted the blanket.

"Good morning, Metin," Trevor Matthews intoned.

"Good morning, sir." He sat and accepted the tumbler of coffee Melanie handed him. The boys trotted over and joined them. Tanner gave him a hug. Zach slapped his shoulder. They ate fruit, cheese, and bread in near total silence. But it felt nice, comfortable, even. At one point, he stared at Melanie as she gazed out over the ocean, holding her water bottle. She glanced at him, and her face broke into a half-smile that set his heart pounding with agony and hope at the same time. He held out a hand. She took it, and they sat connected in a way that transcended any of the sexual encounters they'd shared.

Zach cleared his throat, breaking the moment. "Hey, uh, Metin...?"

"Yeah." He looked at the boy before letting go of Melanie's hand.

"Wanna go...?" He held up the ball.

Metin grinned and jumped up. "Is that a challenge?"

The boy dropped the ball to the sand and dribbled away as an answer.

When Metin glanced at her to see if she was okay with it, Melanie's eyes were filled with tears.

"Thanks for brunch," he said, and she nodded. He tilted her chin up, wiped the tears with his thumb. "We'll talk more, after I go teach your sons a lesson."

. . . .

WHILE THE DAY STARTED out well, it devolved pretty quickly. Zach and Tanner started tussling over the ball right after Metin agreed to ref them. He broke the boys up, sent Zach to jump in the pool to cool off and sat with Tanner who huffed and puffed, near tears.

"It's okay." He put a hand on Tanner's shoulder, surprised when the boy leaned into him and started sobbing into his sweaty T-shirt. He rubbed Tanner's arm and let him finish. Then pretended it never happened so the kid wouldn't be embarrassed before he ran off to torture his older brother some more.

Metin flopped onto his back in the sand, squinting up at the painfully bright blue sky. His chest pounded. His arms itched from being so empty. He needed to drink, or fuck, or something. He sat up fast and almost banged his forehead right into Melanie's. She held out a clean shirt, a ball cap, and a pair of sunglasses.

"Going without sunscreen in this part of the world is ill advised."

He stood, enjoying the cool breeze on his damp skin and the way Melanie eyeballed his bare torso. He took a step closer, relishing the sunscreen, coffee, and vanilla smells of her.

She pushed him away, frowning. "Back off, lover boy. I'm here to talk, or walk, or both. Your call."

"Walking sounds great." He put the clean shirt, hat, and sunglasses on and grabbed her hand before she could protest. She frowned at first. Then twined her fingers in his with a rueful smile. "You gotta be touching all the time, don't you?"

He shrugged. "Is that so bad? I'm pretty good at the touching thing."

"This is a flirt-free zone, mister," she said, drawing an imaginary box around herself with her free hand. "We have some shit to work out and it needs to be sans any touching beyond this." She raised their joined hands.

He smiled, bringing her knuckles to his lips. "Humor me and my need to touch." Rolling her eyes, she asked, "Did Alicia do that?"

He flinched and tried to drop her hand but she gripped it, staring at him so intently he squirmed. "We will talk about her, Metin. It's the only way to figure out if we can get past it. Right now, I'm not sure we can. But if you refuse to talk about her, then forget being around me at all."

His shoulders slumped as anger flared in his chest. Truth she wants? Truth she'll get. "I miss her so much. Every inch, every molecule of me aches every single damn day. I fake it. I pretend that it doesn't, but it does. I drink and it fades. I fuck, and it fades some more. But it is always there. Always." He glared at her. "That enough talking for you? Or do you want to know more?"

She smiled, easing his stress somewhat. "That's a good place to start. C'mon, let's hoof it."

 • • • •

BY THE TIME THEY'D covered nearly three miles down the beach and back, Mel's skin was burned in places she'd missed with the sunscreen, and tears were streaming down her face. It hurt, this forced remembering. But she knew they had to do it.

Metin seemed more and more animated, less surly, as they shared memories of Alicia. Finally, they arrived back at their original picnic spot. The umbrella and the blanket remained, but her dad and the boys were nowhere in sight. She shaded her eyes at the sun and figured it for four p.m. or so.

"I gotta sit." She flopped down under the umbrella. "I feel age spots forming as we speak."

Metin eased down next to her. Their physical proximity was comfortable, easy, and without sexual tension or anything other than the need to share memories. "I have to admit something else," he said, pulling off his shoes and digging his bare toes into the sand. She looked at him and nodded. He took a breath. "Sometimes I wish I could at least have him, Ayden, back. I dream about him every time I sleep. I want to hold him, just one more time and then that would be enough." He sipped from a water bottle she pulled from the cooler. "Then I hate myself for thinking something so awful."

"No, I get that." She said, leaning back on her elbows and keeping her gaze trained out over the water. She felt reamed out, cored, used up and discsarded like a banana skin. Glancing over at him, she realized she now understood his comment about filling the empty space with booze and women. "Damn, I would so take you to bed. I mean right now. Just to make all this stop." Sucking in a huge breath, relieved to be able to admit such a thing, she wiped her face, sick of crying even as she knew she'd never stop mourning her sister. "What have we done, Metin? Why did we? Who do we think we are to just... be...."

He looked at her, one eyebrow raised. "Happy?" he said, his flat voice the opposite of that. "I don't know. You've got me there. We've got a nerve, I guess." His entire body was slumped and defeated, not unlike he'd been when she'd seen him the first time in his Istanbul condo.

She held up a hand. "Here's what I propose." He settled to his side on one elbow, pinning her with his dark gaze. "Cut that out."

"Cut what out?" he asked, running a finger down her bare shoulder.

"Turn off the bedroom eyes, god damn you, and hands off. I mean it." She moved out of his reach. "I hereby officially declare you free of my inner jealous bitch."

He frowned. "Excuse me?"

"Go forth and date women your own age, without the massive load of baggage you and I are lugging around together. It's not healthy for either of us." Her heart broke even as she spoke. But she steeled herself for it—the cold water splash of reality they both needed.

A spark of something resembling anger flashed in his eyes. "You have a hot man waiting in the wings, or what?"

She laughed to cover her need to throw herself at him. "Oh god, no. I'm too busy and too old to date," she insisted. "We weren't dating, in case you didn't notice. We were fucking. A lot, mind you, and it was lovely. But, again, not healthy, and we're stopping now. Okay?"

"Sorry, but no."

"But..."

He got up to stretch and walked towards the water without letting her finish. She gnawed the inside of her cheek as he stripped down to his boxer shorts, the absolute beauty of his lean muscles burning into her retinas. She ached to get her flesh next to his again. He dove in, swam out, then returned, emerging like a god from the sea, the water beading up on his dark skin. Dropping onto the blanket, he shook his hair and sprinkled her with cold droplets. She cursed and swatted his arm.

He grabbed her hand. "Melanie, I love you."

She yanked out of his grip. "No, Metin. You love the fact of me. That I'm here, filling your emptiness. But I'm the wrong person for that. You were married to—you adored—my sister. I can't, I mean I won't, be the second string. You needed something, someone, and I was nearby, convenient and willing. But now we have to face it for what it is—wrong. On too many levels."

"I'm so glad you have me all figured out," he said, grabbing a water bottle. "Good thing somebody does."

She laid a shaking hand on his shoulder, seeking words to soothe them both and coming up short. He moved fast, pinning her under him, kissing her so hard, she barely realized that she kissed him back.

In its usual blend of urgency and erotic perfection, their coming together felt like a contest of wills. But the non-empty sensation was such a relief, every inch of her responded fast, her hair-trigger orgasm tendencies amplified by the final nature of this connection.

"God... yes...." she whispered into his skin as he rocked into her, drawing out a languorous orgasm, completing her, before it all came to a crashing halt.

He came with a groan, shivering and gripping her tight. Propping up on his arms, he spoke, his head bowed. "Please don't do this."

She kissed him once more, with an inner promise it would be the last time, and put her hands alongside his rough face. "I have to. Now get off me before the whole goddamn place catches us."

He sighed and did as she asked. And when he got up and walked away from her, she'd never in her life felt more alone.

That night they sat on the beach, sharing a bottle of red wine and talking, sharing memories of Alicia, even laughing a little at some of their stories. Amazing, she thought as she finished the last of her wine and set the glass back in the basket she'd packed for them. She felt woozy, but not from the booze. All the spent emotions from the last couple of days, including the ill-advised quickie on the beach, plus the sheer overwhelm of their family's loss, made her feel like she was packed in cotton, all sights and sounds and sensations muted.

"I hated you so much," Metin said at one point as she lay with her head in his lap, the wine gone, their moods softened, but somber. He trailed his fingers through her hair as he spoke. "You nearly cost me my son."

"I didn't mean to. It wasn't about you. It was about her." She rolled to her side, facing the ocean, unwilling to revisit that particular topic.

"I know that now. But I hated you. Then." His hand ran down her arm to her waist and hip. "You were so hard to like. And for the record, I think it was about me, or more about how you wanted to prove that you were more important to her—to Alicia—than I ever would be."

"You're probably right about that." Tears fell onto his bare leg. She tasted them, bitter and useless, wishing she'd never opened up this can of worms. Talking about her dead sister felt like grinding a fist full of salt into an open wound.

"But you are an amazing woman. Alicia was lucky to have you as a sister." She sat up, clutching her knees to her chest her face pressed into her knees. "Don't you believe that?"

He had his arm around her as the sobs ripped out from her soul. The years of remaining strong so everyone else could lose it burst open like an overripe watermelon. He held her close, the sensation of his embrace the most perfect thing she'd ever known.

But it was over. Because it had to be.

Chapter Fourteen

Metin watched his date preen and flirt with the waiter, and tried not to roll his eyes. She obviously put a high value on keeping herself looking perfect. But having been married to a woman who sometimes had to be reminded to shave her legs lest he sustain rug burns, he was immune to this sort of behavior. While his date had provided him with pleasant enough distraction for the last few weeks after he'd come home from the holiday with Melanie and her family—Melanie's permission to go forth and date digging a hole into his psyche in a way that made him want to prove something to her — he understood his behavior for what it was.

He hated reverting to type. Being that guy who could never be alone. But he was aware of his own vices and weaknesses, so he'd decided to embrace them. This particular woman had loomed up in his line of vision, and he'd grabbed onto her. Now, she clung to him like cat hair on a dark suit.

Melanie remained his friend, as she'd promised. They spoke two or three times a week, mostly discussing Zach's scholarship offers, her worry over his obsession with his girlfriend, and Tanner's newfound love of basketball.

Metin ate breakfast at the café a lot. He'd made friends with the whole staff, including the lazy bartender Mel could never bring herself to fire because he had a wife and baby and was such a nice guy. He knew he was making excuses to be around her but he couldn't help himself. He loved hearing her laugh, listening to her bitch about the staff, her kids, her house, the dog, anything.

But she insisted on remaining hands off and seemed to mean it this time. So he found someone to keep him company in bed, although if he were honest, he wished the woman would leave afterward. That she'd stop lingering and leaving all her stuff at his house. Tonight, after several weeks of expensive dates and a lot of vigorous, emotionless sex, he got the distinct feeling she expected something from him he was not about to give.

"Listen, Traci, I need to make it an early night. Why don't I take you home and...."

She pouted, leaning forward and providing him an unimpeded view of her ample breasts

This is what you wanted. A bed filler. Now she won't get the hell out of your life. Well played, stud. Well played.

His phone buzzed, so he used the opportunity to stop paying attention to her to check it. A text from Zach. Metin frowned, trying to take in what the kid was saying.

Mom went out on a date tonight. With my biology teacher. Thought you should know.

He frowned and responded: *Your mother is allowed to do whatever she wants. Stop spying on her.*

The boy didn't reply. The low-level buzzing in Metin's ears reached fever pitch by the time he dropped clingy Traci at her place after much cajoling on her part to get him to stay over. He was due to go on a week-long trip with Rafe the next day and couldn't think of anything better than getting some space from this place and everything it represented. They were recruiting coaches for the club team that Jack had whole-heartedly supported, but it meant another level of hiring that he was using as an excuse to distract him from his overall Melanie-pining misery.

He sat in his driveway, composing and erasing several texts to Melanie before deciding that, *"I hear biology teachers really know their way around anatomy. Hope you had a nice date,"* was snarky yet still supportive enough to fly.

He hit send and pressed his forehead against the steering wheel, cursing his lameness, his inability to convince her that he did love her. Double cursing himself for letting her accusations get under his skin. Did he merely need someone, anyone, and Melanie had made herself available to him? And he'd turned around and immediately found Traci to fill that void? Or was he just trying to replace Alicia with someone close to her and would always consider Melanie the second string?

No, that simply wasn't the case. But it seemed his window of opportunity to prove that to her had closed and been painted shut.

She responded within seconds. *I hear sexy ad salesgirls who pretend to be marketing experts give great head.*

He laughed and climbed out of the car and tapped out, *They do.*

When she didn't send anything back after an hour, he tried again, unable to stop. *But there's great, and then there is extraordinary. You are in the latter camp.*

Flatterer, she replied, quickly. *Stop flirting with me. I'm on a goddamned date.*

He decided to go with total honesty: *Okay. Sorry. My date ended early. She bores me to tears anymore.*

Melanie: *Well, sob your way through getting blown. That ought to fix it.*

Metin: *I'll get right on that.*

Nearly two hours passed without another response from her, during which he folded laundry, finished packing, and read some of the material he'd gathered on the coaching prospects they were visiting the following week. Her final text of the night set his teeth on edge, and he used every ounce of willpower not to jump in the car and go to her.

I miss you, she said. *But don't take that the wrong way or anything.*

Metin: *I won't. It's mutual. Headed out to the West Coast tomorrow with Rafe. Will be in touch. Don't do anything I wouldn't with your professor.*

Melaine: *I won't. Goodnight, Metin.*

Metin: *Goodnight, Melanie.*

He smiled and fell asleep on the couch, waking with a start at four a.m. when his alarm went off, then groaned his way through the shower and freezing cold drive to the airport.

• • • •

THE DAYS STRETCHED into weeks and into months, as days will do when they pile in on each other. Mel sleepwalked through most days. Nights remained the opposite of restful. She tossed and turned, read books, watched movies, and managed to snag an hour or three of sleep as morning approached. She was short with her staff and kids.

The rapidity with which she'd let the biology teacher take her out and get into her pants still embarrassed her, but at least it took that particular edge off. Brent Malloy, said biology teacher, was now a fixture in her life and had been for nearly six weeks. They'd consummated the deal a few times in his small condo. It had been fine and had made a slight dent in the raw need she still harbored for Metin.

A handsome, gray-haired, former-researcher-turned-high-school teacher, Brent was divorced, and possessed a self-reliant calm about him that soothed her when it didn't make her feel like a raving banshee. While not exactly shy, more like quiet to the point of invisible, at times he irritated the crap out of her with his tendency to defer to whatever she wanted. But he was a tender, generous lover, so she really had nothing to complain about—a fact she repeated to herself a lot.

Because his demeanor was so opposite of Metin's, she caught herself comparing the two men. After a weekend spent together when the boys were both at camp, she burst into tears at Brent's tidy kitchen table when he'd done nothing more than serve her a picture-perfect breakfast.

"I'm such a bitch," she mumbled, not meeting his eyes. "I don't... I'm not... you are...."

But he'd stopped her with a kiss that progressed quickly into something more, right on the kitchen table. Very Metin-like, and encouraging. But the emptiness she sustained every time she thought about Metin or, after having one of their semi-regular conversations, hurt like a dry tooth socket.

Spring approached and she stayed stuck in a fog of self-denial. Zach was headed to college within months. Tanner had begun devolving from a sweet, supportive boy into his own form of surly teenager, and she missed Metin so badly she'd begun ignoring his calls and texts in order to get past it. Brent kept up his slow, steady, always-there reliability—and had gotten pretty damn good at oral sex now that she'd taught him a thing or three.

Her father's health declined all of a sudden, which only added to her stress. They'd discovered a heart murmur, and she spent a long night in the ER with him just last week, Brent at her side and Metin pacing the hall. At one point, she'd been carrying cups of coffee back for all of them and had stumbled, spilling the stuff everywhere. Metin had grabbed her, held onto her while she cried like a little girl. All in all, par for the Melanie Matthews course, she figured, as she sniveled and pulled away from him when Brent started cleaning up the mess she'd made. Thankfully, Trevor Matthews' heart issue was discovered early, and he was on the mend.

The morning of the day that everything changed, she was sitting, staring into the depths of her coffee mug, when Zach pounded down the hall and past her. "I'll be late tonight, Mom," he called on his way out the door, not giving her time to respond.

She looked at Tanner, hoping for some sign of his former self. But he sat, sulking under a crop of hair in sore need of quality time with a pair of scissors. Ignoring her, he got up and stomped out behind his brother, leaving her alone with her coffee and yet more stupid tears.

* * * *

THAT NIGHT, MEL SAT and tried not to obsess about the time. When it ticked past two a.m. and then two-thirty and she still had no response from Zach, she started pacing. Damn kid knew her rules. If she sent a text, and he didn't respond within thirty minutes, she considered him dead on the side of the road and was calling the cops.

He'd lived with her paranoia long enough to know he should respond immediately, no matter what. She'd sent the first text at one a.m. when she woke from an annoyingly sexy dream starring Metin's lips and tongue.

Groggy, she'd stared at her screen, expecting Zach's usual prompt answer. But it wasn't there. She tried Tanner, who was sleeping over at a friend's house. He sent a message back right away.

He and Gayle broke up tonight, I think. That's the rumor anyway. Let me try a few of his friends.

She re-read that text and her heart skipped a few beats, then began pounding and making her breathless.

After an hour of still nothing from Zach, her panic ramped up by a thousand. She fiddled with her phone, pondering whom she should call. She and Metin still talked, but not as much as they used to, although she'd be happy to hear his voice every day. They were nearly done with Zach's spring season, and Metin had been at every match, causing a fair bit of excitement among the crowd. The boys had one more game before going on to play in the finals, and all signs pointed to them remaining the state champions.

At that moment, she realized and accepted that she needed him, required his presence, to keep her from spinning out into the parental anxiety stratosphere. She sent him a text and sat, drumming her fingers on the tabletop. When nothing appeared in return on the phone screen, she cursed and sent a similar message to Brent at the exact moment she heard a car screech up to the front of her house. Opening the door, she found Metin dressed in a disheveled dress shirt and dark trousers, with a tie loose around his neck. He smelled of strange cologne and sex. She clenched her jaw, determined not to turn this into anything more than it was.

"Have you tried texting Gayle?" He walked past her into the kitchen and grabbed a bottle of water out of her fridge.

"Tanner said they broke up tonight. That's the rumor, and that's why I'm freaking out. We talked about this. He was way too into her. Was bound to get hurt."

"Yeah." Metin sat at the table, calm and quiet. "A boy's first official dumping can be traumatic. I tried calling him after you sent me the text, but it went to voicemail, so his phone is off."

"Shit." Mel sat, her heart pounding and she dropped into the chair next to him.

He laid a hand on her shoulder and she leaned into him, comforted, in spite of herself. "It will be okay."

It was just past four when the police car pulled up. She'd fallen into a fitful sleep against Metin's chest on the couch but she leapt up at the knock, panic beating its wings inside her skull until she spotted Zach standing between the two cops. He kept his gaze down, but he wasn't in handcuffs, thank God. Nor was he dead.

Although he was going to wish he were after they left him with her.

One of the officers filled her in on the call they'd received about a boy sitting on the roof of the high school, throwing empty beer cans down into the parking lot.

"Get inside," Metin said to him before she could say anything, his voice low. "Thank you, officers."

"He didn't blow anywhere near drunk. We think he was pouring the beer out onto the parking lot as well. We had to write him up for destruction of property though, and possession of alcohol by a minor."

Mel clutched her throat and stood back, absorbing this latest disaster, watching the cops get back into their car in her driveway. She turned, speechless with relief.

Zach slouched into the living room, his sweatshirt hood pulled over his eyes. When she caught his eye, she was shocked at the expression on Metin's face, one she could only describe as livid.

"Stand up straight, goddamn you," he said, shocking her. Yanking the boy's hood back. She stepped toward them, willing to hear his story of young heartbreak. Metin's hand shot up in the air, stopping her. "No, Melanie. This is serious. He could lose his scholarships over it."

A small lick of anger at his preemptive behavior with her son replaced her panic about his safety. Zach looked at her, silently begging for her intervention. But she held her tongue.

"Look at me." Metin clamped onto his arm as he spoke in a deep, scary tone. "You worked too hard and your mother has spent too much time and money getting you to this point to start acting like a fool over ..." He paused, glanced at Melanie, then back at Zach. "Do you have any idea how many boys would kill for all the offers you got? And you're prepared to throw that away over what, exactly?"

"Let go of me. You're not my father," Zach said, his blue eyes darkening as he yanked his arm out of Metin's grip. She stepped toward them once more, but Metin held up that annoying, bossy palm again, silencing her and adding fuel to the simmering fury building in her chest.

"No, I'm not. But you will listen to me because I know what I'm talking about." Zach frowned, but Metin kept going. "You do not throw this away because the first girl who let you between her thighs on a regular basis decided to dump you. It's what girls do. You'd better get used to it. Man up, kid. This is the real world where shit falls apart on you at the drop of a hat. I would know. I'm the one who tossed my entire career aside when I shouldn't have."

"Hang on a second." Mel stepped between them. "Metin, you have no right to act like this."

"I have every right, Melanie." His eyes blazed. "You are no better than Alicia was. She coddled my son, let him get away with too much even as a little boy. And this one." He gave Zach another firm shake, "He got the same treatment. You can't let him slide. This is fucking serious."

"Thanks for waiting with me, but you can go now," she said, her voice breaking with emotion.

"Fine." He stepped back from them both. Running a hand through his hair, he said, "Don't ask for my help if you don't want it."

"Sorry I interrupted your... whatever." She gestured to his clothes.

He glared at her. "I had to get re-dressed in a hurry."

She quivered with a choking jealousy, now that she was face-to-face with his new reality. Zach started easing away from them. "I'm not finished with you," she said to him, stopping the boy in his tracks.

Metin's voice was firm. "He needs to email every single coach who extended him an offer, especially Duke, if that's where he's leaning. They'll find out about this and if he doesn't jump in front of it with some kind of explanation...."

Zach's eyes flashed with fear. "Okay, um, I'm gonna go do that, like, right now."

She whipped around to face Metin. "Don't you dare speak to my son like that or bad-mouth my sister in my house. She was a great mother, and you know it." His jaw clenched and Mel froze, wishing the words back even as she kept talking. "She always said that your innate chauvinist pig was close to the surface. That you were too hard on Ayden, trying to make him a man using harsh punishment when he was only two years old. Well, I'm here to tell you that you no longer have to worry about us. You can take anything related to my sons off your radar." She held out a hand to Zach, but he kept his distance, looking between her and Metin, who crossed his arms and glared at her.

"Then why did you text me, if you didn't want my help?"

She shook with fury—mostly at herself. Why was she acting like this? "Go," she ground out, moving away from him, but he grabbed her arm.

Metin set his jaw. "Zach, do you mind? We need to finish this conversation in private."

Zach nodded and slid past them. She stayed frozen in place, focused at the hand Metin had on her. A gut-deep urgency to let him be who he was—what she wanted him to be with her—made her head spin even as her rage at his bossy macho bullshit was making her blood boil. "Go on. Get back to whatever bed you crawled out of."

Without a word, he took her elbow and pulled her gently until they were outdoors, in the overhanging carport next to her SUV. Leaving his hand on her arm he turned her, their bodies so close they might as well be kissing. She averted her face.

"Might I remind you this was your idea. This whole go-forth-and-date-and-we'll-be-friends thing," he said, his voice low. "It was your god damned idea that I agreed with, against my better judgement."

"I don't know what you're talking about." But she did. She had to clench her eyes shut to stop the tears from betraying her.

"I don't want it this way. I want to be with you. Melanie, look at me, damn it."

She opened her eyes once she was sure she wasn't going to cry. "No, you want to be with somebody—anybody will do. You're incapable of being alone. And you only wanted me because...."

Metin made a sound between a growl and a moan. "Stop throwing that in my face as some kind of excuse because you can't cope with how you really feel." He let her go, shaking his head. "I'm sorry I was heavy-handed with Zach. I'm sorry I showed up in my date clothes. But I'm mostly sorry that you are such a colossally stubborn woman that you don't see what's right in front of you. You're not second string, not the replacement sister, none of that shit. I will never, ever stop loving Alicia, Melanie. But she is dead, she and my son are gone from me and will never return. You aren't. You're here. And I love you, you crazy fucking... oh, never mind."

Mel sucked in a breath. Light from the early summer dawn peeked over the horizon, sending rays of pink and orange across the sky. She stared at it a few seconds, then focused back on him.

"I'll tell you what's right in front of me. This man, who was married to my sister, who I hated with every fiber of my being for so long." She held up a hand as he started to interrupt her. "No, listen to me. I did hate you. You fucked with my sister's dream of being a soccer player. Knocked her up not once, but twice." Metin flinched. She didn't let it stop her.

"But I felt bad for you even after that stupid scene at the funeral. And then I was asked to help, so I saw it as a way to redeem myself, to shed a little of the guilt I hauled around for blaming you for her death. And now?" Mel clutched at her arms, frozen by his gaze. "And now... I..." Her heart pounded. She wanted to puke, to run away, to will all the words back into her mouth.

She needed him to force the truth on her, make her see that they could be together and that it would be fine—good, even. But he wasn't going to do that. She had to get to that conclusion on her own and she was already running away from it like a coward.

He was in her space in seconds, holding her, running a finger down her face, his breath hot on her skin as he spoke. "Now we have something else. Something new and something that isn't wrong, or bad, and is even endorsed by your father and your sons. Why won't you accept it?"

She wrenched away from him, chest heaving with the effort to keep her distance. "Because I won't allow myself to love you," she choked out. "I can't. No matter what you say, I'll always feel like you're settling for me." She couldn't believe how petulant and childish she sounded. But it was her core truth.

Metin opened his mouth. She held her breath, hoping against hope he could convince her otherwise. But when another car pulled up to the curb, he frowned.

Brent unfolded his long, lanky frame out of his late model pickup. He didn't rush, and his body language radiated calm as he approached. Metin let go of her and took two steps away, leaving her bereft.

"Him," he whispered. "He isn't wrong for you, perhaps? He won't make you feel like a second stringer?"

She bit her lip, choked with emotion. His eyes flashed.

"Make your choice. But you have to know that I won't wait forever." When Brent walked within earshot, Metin leaned into her ear. "I do love you, Melanie. Deal with it."

Then he shook Brent's hand, gave him a quick rundown of what had happened, and climbed into his sports car without another word or glance in her direction.

Chapter Fifteen

Metin sat behind the bench to watch the Michigan high school state championship match as Zach's team took the field and controlled the entire first half of the match. He'd spotted Melanie with Brent as they filed into the University's soccer complex at the same moment her eyes found his. Wishing he could avoid it, but knowing it had to be done, he made his way over to them.

Melanie gave him a perfunctory hug, smiled in an almost-but-not-quite genuine way. They hadn't spoken or exchanged texts since the night of Zach's arrest. Although he stayed in touch with Zach about the fallout afterward, he refused to discuss anything other than soccer with the boy. He'd stopped eating breakfast at Ayden's Café and focused his attention instead on the team and himself. He also tried a little experiment and stopped going out with the clingy girl. He didn't give in to temptation to ask out a different one either, accepting that being alone was something he should work on, for his own sake.

Now that he had his full head and heart around their last few months, he felt nothing but good about the time he'd shared with Melanie. Other than how he had screwed it up somehow, making her feel guilty about her own need for him. He understood her personality well enough by now to know she wouldn't allow herself to admit what she wanted. No matter what he did, he wouldn't be able to convince her he'd be anything but settling for her—that he wanted to be with her forever, for herself, not because she represented a connection to Alicia he couldn't shake.

Memories of Alicia bombarded him still—getting worse, if anything. Not in a guilty way but in a way that made him even more convinced that he had missed out, had fucked up his second chance at love. A love much different from his first—less intense, but just as crucial to his happiness.

Miles of running, swimming at the YMCA, watching film with Rafe, going on recruiting trips, and formulating strategy with Parker and Nicco took most of his time. And when he wasn't doing that, he was working on setting up the fee-free club program with Jax. He stayed busy. And while he felt stronger or more in control of himself than ever, the sharp spike of jealousy piercing him between the eyes at the sight of a classy diamond ring on Melanie's left hand had left him breathless. He shook Brent's hand and moved away from them before punching anybody's lights out—his first inclination.

And so he sat, brain boiling, his gaze drawn to the two of them over and over, sitting close, laughing, talking to other parents when they weren't cheering. He kept quiet during the game like he usually did, not wanting Zach's coach to think he was there to usurp authority. But as the game went scoreless into the eightieth minute, he noticed something about one of the team's midfielders.

"Hey," he whispered to the coach. "I think number ten is hurt." Any player worth a damn wouldn't ask to come out for any reason, especially at a match like this one. But he was having more and more trouble disguising some kind of an injury. The coach narrowed his eyes at the kid limping and wincing.

Unable to stop himself, Metin leaned close again. "Pull Zach to mid, push number twenty-two up top. You need more control in the middle, and Zach knows where to place the ball—I taught him," he said. "I mean, you know, for what it's worth."

The coach's pointed look ran along the lines of Mind Your Own Fucking Business You Washed Up Has-Been, but he did exactly as Metin suggested. It was brutally hot for June, and all the boys were gassed by that point in the frustrating, physical, defensive game.

Zach glanced over at him when the player substition was made. Metin gave him a nod. They'd worked on this. Setting up the right player to score was as important as the actual act, especially late in a stressful match. He'd been a quick study and was headed into Division

1 scholarship soccer, likely as a midfielder. So this needed to come as second nature to him. The play resumed.

He batted the ball around at his feet, cut left, and sent a high arcing pass to the newly promoted forward, who fumbled it, sending it to the left of the goal. But the goalkeeper had made the crucial error of contact with it, forcing a corner kick for Zach's team, presenting one of the best opportunities to score they'd had for the entire game. Metin leaned forward, willing the kid to remember what they'd practiced.

Zach moved into position, right outside the net. When the kicker gained the advantage, he shifted to the right to receive the pass and leapt into the air. A second after the exact moment Zach executed a textbook header into the goal for the score, his forehead collided with the back of the goalkeeper's skull. The crowd gasped in alarm as both boys hit the turf hard, then lay unmoving.

Metin jumped to his feet, heart in his throat. Melanie stood, hand to her mouth, while everyone around her sat. Zach's team celebrated until realizing he was still down. The goalkeeper sat up, rubbing and shaking his head. Zach still hadn't moved. The formerly raucous crowd stayed silent. Metin walked out onto the field, slow and steady, not wanting to give away how panicked he was at the sight of Zach's immobile body. He knelt down across from the trainer who'd run out already and touched the goose egg sprouting on the boy's forehead.

"Zach," he whispered.

"I'm getting the stretcher out here," the trainer declared after attempts to revive the kid failed. Metin nodded, not taking his eyes off Zach's unconscious face.

When the trainer motioned for the EMTs who had an ambulance parked nearby, Zach opened one eye. "Is she coming out?" he asked under his breath.

Surprise replaced panic, which was quickly supplanted by fury when Metin glared at the supine kid. "What the hell are you talking about?" He looked up when Melanie appeared at his side. She shook so hard, her teeth chattered as she put her hand on Zach's forehead.

"Metin, my god is he okay?"

Unable to stop himself, Metin put his arm around Melanie's shoulders. She pressed her face into his neck. "He's going to be okay." He allowed himself a small kiss to her hair, adoring the familiar smells, and the sensation of torso against his.

The EMTs rolled out the stretcher and lifted Zach onto it. When the boy raised one hand with a thumbs-up, the crowd began to cheer. Metin stopped the stretcher when Melanie was out of earshot and leaned down close to Zach's ear. "Even I wouldn't do this, especially not to my own mother. Now I know you need a CT scan."

Zach nodded. "It really hurts. And I'm, like, seeing double," he croaked out. Melanie, who'd appeared at Metin's elbow, gasped at the sound of her son's words.

"Honey, are you okay?"

"Yeah, Mom." He winced as the stretcher bounced to the sidelines. "I want Metin to come to the hospital with us."

Metin shrugged, but his heart beat a funny rhythm in his chest at Melanie's proximity.

"Sure, baby, whatever you want," she said. They watched as Zach was wheeled off the field and loaded into the waiting ambulance.

"I'll drive us," the damned biology teacher, who had materialized at some point, declared.

The man's gangly presence irritated the shit out of him. But he tried not to let it show. Melanie stood between them, her eyes on Metin. Brent put a proprietary arm around her shoulder, his brown gaze sending a distinct message of "back off, this one's not yours anymore." Metin took a step farther away. They all flinched when the ambulance squealed out of the parking lot.

"I can drive all of us," the biology teacher declared, his mature calm like fingernails on Metin's inner chalkboard. Then the man turned

Melanie slowly, but firmly, away from him. They climbed into big SUV, and Metin watched, his heart sinking to his knees.

That's it. She'd made her decision, like he'd told her to. He climbed behind the wheel of his sports car, cranked rap music, and got in the line behind the ambulance, frozen with remorse.

Epilogue

Two years later

"Oh god, make it stop." Mel rolled over and pulled the pillow over her head. Exhaustion lit every corner of her being. "Did Tanner ever come home?" she mumbled from her soundproof haven. Even as she tried not to, she took a quick mental inventory of her loved ones.

Zach had begun his second year playing soccer at Georgia Tech, since Duke revoked his scholarship offer, thanks to the concussion scare. Tanner had assumed the role of Problem Son with gusto. Late nights, illicit house parties, and surly attitudes interspersed with yelling arguments about the state of his room, his grades, and his pot head friends were part and parcel of life with that kid. Where her sweet, happy little boy had gone, she had no idea.

"Yeah." Her husband rolled away from her. "I stayed up to make sure he met the curfew."

"Thanks." She sighed, grateful for a lot of reasons. He was so sturdy and calm in the face of Tanner's scary descent into wild, teenage boyhood.

"I'll get this one," he said. She peeked at the clock—five a.m. on a Saturday. Though so bone-tired in body and mind, and slightly ill contemplating it, she needed to get in to the café that morning, since her general manager was out sick. She watched as he pulled on a pair of jeans and ran a hand through his hair. "Get another hour, Mel. You had the last shift." Giving her leg a pat, he yawned and then wandered out into the hall.

She drifted off, her over-taxed brain dropping directly into deep sleep, only to be startled awake by smelly dog breath. Opening one eye, she stared at the animal's huge face on the bed next to her. Noting an hour and a half had passed since she'd last seen the clock, she sat up. The house was silent. Staggering a little, she hit the shower, emerged, dressed, and wandered into the hall, still in a haze of exhaustion.

"Coffee. I need lots and lots of coffee," she said, padding down the hallway toward the kitchen.

Stopping at the door of Zach's old room, she smiled at the sight of the tiny baby girl nestled into her father's neck. She watched them both sleep for a few minutes, marveling at how close she'd come to making the wrong decision—to choosing the life that seemed right over the one that she truly wanted.

The baby stirred, snorted around, made a small mewling cry. Mel's breasts responded in kind, tingling and leaking. "Ow," she yelped. "Wake up, you lazy shit. I gotta feed your spawn."

The man opened his eyes and grinned at her, his face a mask of pure joy as he stood, handed their daughter into her arms, and guided her down to the seat.

"This whole baby thing was a bad idea, you know." She winced when Ava latched onto her nipple with a healthy tug. "I never should have let you talk me into it."

The baby flinched when a tear dropped on her face, but didn't let it distract her from her singular mission.

Her husband crouched down next to her, ran his finger along the girl's cheek, then Mel's breast. Her eye caught the glint of the thin gold ring he wore, an exact match to hers. "I'm pretty convincing when I want to be," he said, leaning over the milky-smelling baby to kiss her lips.

"Yeah," Mel said, yawning and putting her forehead against his, her heart calm and her soul sated. "You are."

"I love you," Metin whispered, kissing her hair.

"Good thing, since you're just another in a line of men who knocked me up."

"Yeah, but I'm the end of that line now," he said, fake frowning. "We clear on that?" He put a protective hand around the back of her neck, soothing her.

"Crystal."

. . . .   .

IT ONLY TOOK A COUPLE of weeks after Zach's concussion all clear for her to return to him, no longer wearing the biology teacher's engagement ring. She'd found him in the backyard of a house he'd purchased not far from hers, kicking balls into a goal after a ten-mile run, contemplating what would possibly be next for him. The hole that Alicia and Ayden's deaths ripped into his soul would never be healed. He knew that. And although Melanie was more than a mere filler, he also knew he would never convince her of that.

When he looked up, sweat dripping from his hair, she was standing on his patio in a pretty yellow sundress, her face wearing a grim expression.

"I'm here to tell you something." Waiting for another lecture, more curses and whatever else she needed to get off her chest, he stood, silent but for the whooshing sound of his pulse in his ears. "I love you. But don't get a big head over it or anything."

He grinned, and the icy cage around his heart began to thaw. "I won't, but you have to tell me something else." He made his slow, determined way across the lawn to her, his soul lifting with every step. She seemed to shrink in on herself as he approached. But when he touched her arm, then pulled her close and kissed her, she relaxed in his embrace. He broke the kiss reluctantly, cradling her face with shaking hands.

"What else did you want to know?" she whispered.

He chuckled. "You know what? I forgot. Well, there is this." He clutched her ass, trailing a hand up to her breast. He buried his nose in her neck. "Say it again," he muttered, eyes closed, not willing to believe it yet.

"I love you, Metin. Now take me inside and prove how happy you are to hear it."

He did exactly that for a day or two at least. Then they went to the courthouse, signed a paper, exchanged rings, and made their announcement at a small party in Ayden's Café.

Her father cried for the first time since his own wife died. Metin's family showed up en masse from Turkey to surprise them all.

And it was, if not perfect, then pretty damn close.

The End

I'll be offering the RED CARD prequel (Metin and Alicia's story) via my newsletter only.

Be sure to subscribe so you won't miss out!

Click here to subscribe![1]

---

1. https://www.subscribepage.com/houserulestwo

Let's move on now that we have our head coach's life sorted, shall we?

Dive into the Black Jack Gentlemen Book 2: SHUT OUT

Here's a taste of the meet cute:

Sophie kept her chair turned from the office door, unwilling to acknowledge the next soccer player awaiting her. She was sweaty and exhausted, with a blinding afternoon low-caffeine headache. Talking these over-paid, over-sexed, full-of-themselves prima donnas through their final contracts and benefits packages didn't help one bit. However, as head of legal for the team in its third year, she had a new crop of new players to orient—ten, to be exact.

But if one more of them waltzed in, reeking of sweat and staring at her as if she were the last crumb on the cookie tray, their flirty high beams blazing—so help her. As if she'd ever be interested in any of their little boy preening. For the thousandth time, she questioned her sanity, taking on this utter crapshoot of a project.

She closed her eyes a moment, shutting down her natural reaction to ponder the reasons, poke at them, rip off the scab that had more or less healed over them in her desperate attempt to start over.

"Hey," a deep, syrupy-sounding voice intoned, sending a strange tremor straight down her spine. "Um, am I in the right place?" It hit her ears as: 'm ah in the raht playce?

She swiveled around and shoved her glasses up her nose to get a good look at the next player looming in her doorway, taking in his jet-black hair, the strong lines of his stubbled jaw, and the breadth of his T-shirt clad shoulders. The Black Jack Gentlemen wore gray when they practiced, their uniforms provided by a famous Detroit-based casino, its logo emblazoned across the front. And said shirt clung to the sculptured torso, blocking her doorway in a way that ought to be outlawed. All the while, Mr. Southern Accent stood stock still, as if used to being so frankly appraised.

A drop of sweat formed at her temple. She resisted the urge to wipe it away. He cleared his throat, so she jerked her gaze up to a set of the darkest eyes she had ever encountered. He smiled—a sweet, lopsided thing that imprinted itself on her brain in a wholly annoying way.

"Hey... uh... I'm Brody. Brody Vaughn." He ran fingers through his hair, nervousness as bright as a neon sign over his head.

Adorable. Her radar pinged like mad. But she forced it to shut the hell up. She had no business thinking about these kids in any way other than purely professional.

So far, they had all been the exact same breed of cocky assholes, alternating between eye-fucking her and extreme boredom in response to her monotonous drone of legalese. Sexy Southern Accent— "Brody," she muttered under her breath—put his hand out, as if to shake hers. His face reddened charmingly when she raised an eyebrow at his outstretched palm—the same one he'd just dragged through his sweat-soaked hair.

She rose slowly to her feet, needing to be at his level. He blinked, then dropped into the chair opposite hers without a word. Sophie took a long, calming breath, forcing herself to focus in ways she had learned, practiced, utilized in her years as a professional Dominatrix—a woman who took money in exchange for bringing pain and raw, rough sex to the men who requested her services.

As she shut the door, keeping her back to the boy—to Brody who was not much more than a boy—her pulse continued to race. Her heart pounded out its disconcerting rhythm, no matter what tricks she employed, which pissed her off. And that, finally, calmed her enough to face him.

"Hello, Mr. Vaughn. I'm Sophie Harrison, legal counsel for the Black Jack Gentlemen. I'll be explaining the terms of the contract you or your agent negotiated with our organization." She talked, using words she'd said a hundred times already. But her own voice echoed around in her head. She focused on the paper in front of her, irritated by her glasses, which kept sliding down her nose. All the while ignoring the raw, visceral reaction her body and brain were having to the man across from her—Brody, a twenty-six-year-old man, his player fact sheet stated.

No, he is a boy, and you don't play with boys—not anymore.

She compressed her lips, pretending to find a nonexistent problem with the stack of legal documents pertaining to his agreement. To his credit, he stayed silent and still, in a way that intrigued her.

Finally, she met his gaze once more and blinked—then frowned. "So, another goalkeeper?" she asked, fully aware how it would needle the average, ego-driven, high-level athlete. A glimpse at his salary indicated his golden-child status. So this was the keeper the club had managed to sign, thanks to the aggressive recruiting activity by their assistant coach.

She tried out a casual smirk but discarded it. The way he looked at her as if memorizing her brought a hot flush to her cheeks. Straightening, she sucked in a breath and forced her thoughts to her next real workout—the kind she preferred that involved tight leather, her favorite bullwhip and a willing submissive.

"You okay there, Miz Harrison?" His voice slithered around in her brain, nestling in nice and low, gripping the base of her skull and making her want to jump up and run out of the room. She glared at him.

"I'm fine." After shoving her glasses back up her nose, she slapped the contracts down in front of him, probably a little too hard. She needed Mr. Brody Vaughn the hell out of her office. She attempted to use her neutral face, to not snarl or growl or snap the poor kid's head off.

He shifted in his seat, cleared his throat, and glanced down at the papers she'd pinned under her manicured fingers, giving her a rush of control over the situation. Her spine tingled in a familiar way, but she channeled it—recognizing the distinct, loose, fluid feeling of compulsion.

"Now, let's go through this." She glanced down at her desk. His hand covered hers. Surprised, she flinched, and a strange, embarrassing sound emerged from her throat.

"I think you need a drink of water. You seem a little done in." His deep drawl coated her nerves like the sweetest honey-infused bourbon.

She snatched her water bottle, gulped some, and took a breath. Within thirty minutes she had laid out the terms of the contract, including his non-disclosure and good-behavior clauses, the health insurance guarantees, all of it. These kids had highly paid agents who'd likely been over it with him, but she wanted to do it to, to ensure there were no misunderstandings.

He asked a few questions, his voice soft, musical, and soothing in a way that had the opposite effect on her nerves. She gritted her teeth against the urge to lock the door and yank the kid's sweaty clothes off.

Jesus, help me. Get him out of here.

He rose quickly, startling her. "Well, if that's it."

She got to her feet, unwilling to look up at him at first and then noting how his chocolate brown eyes appeared to darken even further when she faced him.

"Yes. That will definitely be... ah ... it." Wincing at her squeaky voice, she willed her knees to stop shaking. She would have little reason to see him ever again, unless he landed in trouble and she had to handle a legal problem on his behalf.

His physical presence, not that different from all the others who'd paraded through there in the last few days, compelled her in ways she refused to acknowledge. He stood nearly six-foot-six, which made sense, given his position on the team. His broad shoulders, narrow waist, long, strong legs, filled her brain.

He cleared his throat. And the traitorous flush crept up her neck to her face again. His angular features at that moment were set, and bored, perhaps a touch amused at her obvious discomfort. She narrowed her gaze. Why hadn't she noticed it before? Her pulse fluttered as she put a hand to her throat.

As if reading her mind, Brody Vaughn lifted his chin slightly, and she got a good look at the black chain imprinted at the base of his neck. A dark, circular pattern of interlocking, heavy loops was inked onto tanned flesh. He smiled again. It was slow moving like his drawl. He touched the ink once, then turned, giving her a breathtaking rear view of the chain as he walked toward the office door.

The man wore a collar, a permanent one. But the vibes he threw her proclaimed one thing loud and clear: the person who'd bestowed the collar no longer had any claim on him.

Her mind swooped, whirled, and doubled around on itself, picturing him—Brody, the man—at her knees, bound, and awaiting her command. She shivered and jumped when her assistant appeared at the door. Brody had left, trailing that mysterious aura of vulnerability and strength behind him.

· · · ·

SHUT OUT IS A STORY of rough backstories and backgrounds, the politics of concussions in pro sports, and of second chances.

NOW you really should dive into the series that started it all, The Stewart Realty Series!

It is best enjoyed in this order:

Floor Time

Sweat Equity

Closing Costs

Dual Agency

Escalation Clause

Conditional Offer

Mutual Release

Backup Offer

Good Faith (This novel is not a romance but a 2nd generation novel with plenty of romantic elements. Please read the content warnings before you start).

About Liz Crowe

· · · ·

LIZ CROWE IS A KENTUCKY native and graduate of the University of Louisville living in South Carolina. She's spent her time as a three-continent expat trailing spouse, mom of three, real estate agent, brewery owner and bar manager, and is currently a digital marketing and fundraising consultant, in addition to being an award-winning author.

The Liz Crowe backlist has something for any reader seeking complex storylines with humor and complete casts of characters that will delight and linger in the imagination long after the book is finished.

Her favorite things to do when she's not scrolling social media for cute animal videos is walk her dogs, cuddle her cats, and watch her favorite sports teams while scrolling social media for cute animal videos.

Follow along with Liz online at lizcrowe.com

Sign up for her newsletter at lizcrowe.com

Follow/ like @lizcroweauthor on Facebook, Instagram, Twitter, TikTok

Don't miss out!

Visit the website below and you can sign up to receive emails whenever Liz Crowe publishes a new book. There's no charge and no obligation.

https://books2read.com/r/B-A-ZHTD-XXLED

BOOKS 2 READ

Connecting independent readers to independent writers.